RACHEL POLLACK

Winner of the
World Fantasy Award
Arthur C. Clarke Award
Nominated for the
Nebula Award
Locus Award
Mythopoeic Award
Tiptree Award
Gaylactic Spectrum Aw
Lambda Award

"'The Beatrix Gates' is a stunning study in identity and mutability. It can be read most easily as a story about transexualism or simply a powerful examination of difference and its more positive consequences, as well as a subtle investigation of exactly what makes our identities."
—*Green Man Review*

"Brilliantly original, funny, and fascinating. . . . Pollack turns the world on its spiritual head."
—*Kirkus Reviews*

"'The Beatrix Gates' is a marvelous example of how sci-fi can remythologize the terms of common experience to elucidate and give new and deeper meaning."
—*Lambda Book Report*

The
Beatrix
Gates

plus

PM PRESS OUTSPOKEN AUTHORS SERIES

PM PRESS OUTSPOKEN AUTHORS SERIES

The Beatrix Gates

plus

The Woman Who Didn't Come Back

plus

Trans Central Station

and much more

Rachel Pollack

PM PRESS | 2019

"The Woman Who Didn't Come Back" first appeared in *More Tales from the Forbidden Planet*, ed. Roz Kaveney, Titan Books, 1990
"Burning Beard" first appeared in *Interfictions*, eds. Delia Sherman and Theodora Goss, Interstitial Arts Foundation, 2007
"The Beatrix Gates" first appeared in *The Future Is Queer*, eds. Richard Labonté and Lawrence Schimel, Arsenal Pulp Press, 2006
"Trans Central Station" is original to this volume and this universe

The Beatrix Gates
Rachel Pollack © 2019
This edition © PM Press
Series Editor: Terry Bisson

ISBN: 978-1-62963-578-1
LCCN: 2018931528

Cover design by John Yates/www.stealworks.com
Author photograph by Rubi Rose
Insides by Jonathan Rowland

PM Press
P.O. Box 23912
Oakland, CA 94623
www.pmpress.org

10 9 8 7 6 5 4 3 2 1

CONTENTS

The Woman Who Didn't Come Back

IN THE OLD DAYS, when a woman died, she returned to life after nine days.

On the first day after her death her friends laid her body on her bed. They tied ribbons around the hands and feet and placed a stone over the mouth. Then they would sit around the bed, as silent as their dead sister. Those who were bored, or sore, or hadn't liked the dead woman very much, told themselves they would need the same thing done for them someday. And they kept sitting.

On the second day they got up and cooked, their first hot food in twenty-four hours. When they were sitting round the bed again, they began to speak, telling what they knew about the woman. They told of favors she'd done them, fights they'd had with her. Someone might tell how the woman had nursed her when she had the flu, another how the woman had cheated her when they'd shared a house. They told whatever they could remember, the whole day long. The third day they buried her.

On the fourth, fifth, and sixth days they took care of their sister's business, paying her debts, writing letters for her, selling old clothes and useless junk, leaving only the things she would need for starting over. If the woman had enemies, some of the friends put on masks of her face and visited the people, doing what they could to satisfy the anger. When they got tired they reminded themselves of a woman named Carla, who had made so many enemies before her death it seemed like half the women in town were putting on masks and visiting the other half.

On the seventh and eighth days they prepared for the party. They hung banners in the woman's colors, they decorated the bar with her picture, they cooked or baked all her favorite foods. They cleaned and polished the bar, the furniture, and even the silverware. They set out baskets of flowers up and down the street.

On the ninth day they paraded from the woman's house to the bar, setting out at sundown with drums and whistles, arriving just as the last sigh of daylight faded from the sky. Then the party began. It went on for hours, everyone getting drunk or stoned, playing the woman's favorite records, until all of a sudden, when it seemed they'd forgotten about the woman herself, the door opened and there she stood.

The returned women always came in slightly wet, hair damp and curly, skin glistening. They walked inside and looked around, and everyone stopped, the only noise coming from a record player, or someone who'd tripped against a table or knocked over a glass.

After a moment someone would rush up with a drink, someone else with a roll baked in the shape of the Earth and covered with poppy seeds. As soon as the woman had taken a sip and a bite everyone started to talk again. But the nervousness would last, people spilling drinks or banging into each other. For there was something they had to do, even though no one knew why. Finally one of the younger women would go up to the returned woman and say to her, "What was it like?"

The woman would think a moment, maybe look away. "Sorry," she'd say, "I'm not allowed to tell you that." And then all the women would go back to dancing and getting drunk.

Sometime in the late evening, just as everyone was thinking it was time to go home, the woman who had come back would look around the room and see someone, maybe an ex-lover, maybe someone she'd never noticed before. She would ask her to dance. When the two of them had gone off together the party could end.

Sometimes the couple stayed together for months, even years, sometimes just for a night or a few days. But always, as the returned woman left the bar, holding on to her lover, something like a breeze would pass across her face, and she would stop for a moment, squinting, or tilting her head, like someone trying to remember something. Then her friend would pull on her arm and they'd go home together. Later, if anyone asked her "What was it like?" she'd shrug, or shake her head. "Don't know," she'd say. "Can't remember."

For a long time this went on. Then one day a woman named Marjorie drowned when her boat smashed against a rock. Her friends built a stone circle at the water's edge and asked the sea to return her body. When it washed ashore they took it home and laid it on the bed.

Nine days later Marjorie returned, wearing yellow pants and a loose black shirt over her low breasts. A tall woman with thick shoulders and veined hands and long black hair, she stood in the doorway, wet and shining like the morning. It was strange to see her without glasses. No one had ever seen Marjorie without glasses before. The dead always returned with perfect vision, though it only lasted a few days before the world began to blur again.

Marjorie took a roll and a glass of bourbon. A few minutes later Betty, a neighbor of hers, asked her, "What was it like?" Marjorie threw up her hands and laughed. "Sorry," she said, "secret."

All evening Marjorie danced about the room or sat trading stories with her former lovers. As it got late people started looking at each other, wondering when they could leave. Finally, Marjorie spotted someone, a young woman named Lenni. A newcomer, Lenni leaned against the pool table, drinking a bottle of beer. She was thin, with narrow hips and long fingers. She wore tight black pants and yellow boots and a blue silk shirt and silver chain with a black crescent around her neck. She tilted back her head to finish the beer, and when she brought down her eyes there was Marjorie.

"Want to dance?" the returned woman said.

Lenni had just broken up with a woman named Berenice. Berenice was so beautiful that some people said the Moon faded and then hid for three days a month because she couldn't compete with Berenice. And Marjorie had a slight scar on her left cheek below the ear, where a lover had cut her with a ring. So when Marjorie asked Lenni to dance, Lenni stared down at her empty bottle and shook her head.

No one in the room made a sound.

"Do you want to dance?" Marjorie asked again.

"I'm sorry," Lenni said, so low she could hardly hear her own voice. "Maybe another time."

Marjorie stood up straight. She ran her fingers through her still damp hair. All her life Marjorie had hated it whenever anyone told her no. She'd gone sailing and smashed her boat because a woman named Kathleen had told Marjorie she couldn't see her anymore. Now Marjorie stared at Lenni until the younger woman tried to walk away. Marjorie blocked her. "Why won't you dance with me?" she said.

Lenni shrugged. "I don't want to," she said. And then she smirked.

Jayne, who was running the bar that night, ran up to take Marjorie's arm. "Come on," she said, "let's dance."

Marjorie pulled loose her arm. "Shut up," she said. To Lenni she demanded, "Why don't you want to dance with me?"

Lenni crossed her arms. She looked Marjorie up and down and then she smiled.

Marjorie clenched her fists. She opened them and wiped her hands on her jeans. "Do you want to know what it was like?" she said. "Do you want me to tell you what it was like?" Lenni tried to slide away, but Marjorie grabbed her arm. When Jayne tried to separate them, Marjorie shoved her aside.

Marjorie told Lenni and all the others everything that happened to her. She told them of a dark room, so large she couldn't see the walls, only a green floor and high above her a yellow ceiling. She told them of the sound of wings, and birds crying, of a cold wind shaking her body, cleaning off the smell of the sea. She told them of laughter and scuffling feet, and voices, as if the whole room was filled with people, but when she tried to see them she could only get a kind of afterimage in the dark—people lying together, or dancing in each other's arms. And then she was opening a red door and walking up stone steps with nothing on either side but a noise of grinding rocks. She became sluggish, afraid her unbalanced lump of a body would tilt backwards and roll down the stairs. And then something brushed her face, and she panicked and began to run . . .

The story went on, while some of the women covered their ears or banged on the tables. Lenni stood there, her arms folded, her chin down, her eyes tilted up. Only when Marjorie had finished, when all the other women fell silent again, only then did Lenni and Marjorie take a step back, staring like lovers who've goaded each other into some undesired act of violence. Marjorie turned around, saw all the frightened faces. "Shit," she said, "I wasn't supposed to do that."

"Marjorie?" Lenni said. She took a step towards her. Marjorie ran for the door, slipping once on a pool of beer. Just as she reached the street she heard Lenni shout something. She turned around.

In the bar the women heard a horn and screech of brakes. When they rushed outside Marjorie lay dead.

For the next nine days the women followed all the customs. But on the first day they found it hard to keep silent, and on the second found it even harder to come up with something to say. After they'd buried her, no one could think of anything to do, anything they wanted to fix, any people they wanted to see. Jayne thought of putting on a mask of Marjorie and visiting Lenni. But she kept postponing it, and postponing it, until the sixth day had passed and it was too late.

On the seventh day they did nothing. On the eighth they hung a few banners and bought some cake, but no one polished anything or put out any baskets of flowers. And on the ninth evening only a few women walked together to the bar, and when a couple tried to sing something the others didn't join in and they stopped after a single verse.

The party went on until dawn, but there wasn't much celebrating. The only woman who'd bought any new clothes was Lenni, dressed in red silk trousers and a long yellow shirt, with spangled green running shoes. But Lenni only stood in the back, leaning against the pool table with a bottle of beer in her hand. The women stayed until dawn. When they saw the sky brighten, and people walking to work, they knew that Marjorie would never walk through the door, would never stand before them, her skin glistening with water and light.

From that day no one who dies has ever come back.

The Beatrix Gates

Do you remember cancer? In the old days people fought long heroic battles with it, usually in a scorched-body campaign. Destroy enough tissue and the cancer will run out of food and shrivel away. When the original Nano Factory came up with the first cancer nannies the designers gave them to doctors who fitted them out like miniscule robo-soldiers and sent them off to war. Cut and burn. Cell by cell. Retake the ground and wall off the infected village, kill the organs in order to save them.

Then it struck someone. Maybe we'd misunderstood cancer. Maybe cancer was the body's desire to become immortal. Cancer cells refused limits, refused to decorously die. They invaded wherever they could go, wherever the medical empire couldn't firebomb them. So over the outrage of the doctors the Factory (already partly in the hands of the Revolution) began to send in nannies to run with the cancer insurgency. See what cancer really wants, see how we could use it to overthrow the body's commitment to limits and death. Out of this campaign came the Immortalist program, with all its possible bodies no one ever thought of.

The someone who first saw all this was Annie O, one of the Ancient Trannos, that group of us who managed to survive the rapturous leap into the new world of unlimited nano-transformo. In the old days, Annie was the secret king of America. A homegrown Kansas transgirl, a Colorado Biber Baby (named for the cowboy doctor and his sex change clinic in the Plains town of Trinidad), Annie had a brief career as a transgender terrorist before she discovered the hijras of India, the world's oldest ongoing trans religion. She arrived in Delhi just as hijras were starting to win seats in Parliament under the platform "Men have fucked up and women too, so why not try something else?" Like some sort of trans anthropologist, Annie came to film and take notes. She stayed to put on a sari and dance in the streets. She'd already passed the hijra initiation test—"made the cut," as someone once put it—and the hijras embraced her American trans-formed body, sending her back as king to an America that had no idea it needed one.

Annie could see cancer in a different way because she understood desire. The desire to die and the desire to live, entwined like two snakes around a tree older than the world. This is the tranno secret, that we are not just willing to die, we long for it, passionately, as the pathway to life. Cut open, emptied out, boiled and cleaned and reassembled. These are old stories, from long before the Nanochine Society took over the Factory and began to get it right, creating new people out of old longings.

Do you know about the birth of Aphrodite? Ouranos, the Sky, was hurting the Earth, Gaia. Actually, he was suffocating her and killing all their children. Clever Gaia managed to save one of their kids, Kronos, and as soon as he was old enough, Momma gave him a stone sickle and told him to take care of Daddy. Kronos didn't go for Pop's throat. He aimed further down and cut off Ouranos Jr. and threw it into the sea. Ouranos gave up after that. The Sky pulled back a safe distance from the ground, crossed only by birds and rockets, neutrinos and weather nanos. But those missing pieces—they stirred up a torrent of foam on the water and out of that foam stepped Aphrodite the Passionate. This is a very old story.

Here is another one. Osiris, gentle God of Egypt, inventor of beer, brother-sister of Isis (who Is and is, forever and ever), lover of sister Nepthys, the Goddess of alchemical mud, Osiris was also brother and brother-in-law of Set, a nasty piece of work if ever there was one. Jealous like Iago, Set chops his brother into fourteen pieces and hides them all over the world. Isis, never one to give up easily, searches up and down the old creation until she can reassemble her jigsaw puzzle husband. Only, there's one part missing. A hungry fish has gulped down the penis and dropped down to the oozy black at the bottom of the Nile. So what's a wife (and sister) to do? Isis creates the world's first—everything in myth is first, that's the point of myth—Isis creates the world's first strap-on. With the help of a God named Thoth, inventor of writing, science, magic, and Everything Worth Knowing, this wooden cock crows Osiris back to life.

This is what we mean when we say "sex change." Ripped apart, cut to pieces, and put back together. You have to want it. All of it.

And Thoth, the God of geeks—if the name sounds familiar, it should. You know the ibis nano-tattoo on the upper thigh that marks someone as a member of the Nanochine Society? You know how some nons talk about fucking a trannie as "entering the Palace of the Ibis"? That ibis is Thoth. The Egyptian scrolls depicted the God as a bird-headed techie writing on papyrus. Sometimes the old Gods don't die, they just keep busy until humanity catches up with them. In the ancient world, Thoth revived the dead, he taught the secret sciences, he steered the boat of heaven through the sky and the dark underworld. Sound familiar? When the nannies launch their expeditions into your cells, it's Thoth who guides them. When you pass through the nano Cloud of Unknowing, and you hear that distant flutter of wings, that's Ibis-Thoth.

Dismemberment. Trans (trance) formation. The desire to die is the desire to live. Cancer, the desire to live forever. It took a tranno terrorist street dancer to see it.

As they say in the Society, let's not beat around the burning bush (and if you can't figure out a bush that burns without being consumed, well, honey, there may be no hope for you). The nons—the non-transsexuals—who first built the Factory wanted their nan-o-ma-chines to make them *better*, to cure their sicknesses and keep them young, and make everyone pretty, but not actually *different*. They didn't want to stop being who they were, or thought they were, to become something seriously new. And they didn't understand why their tiny machines seemed to come up against unexpected limits, why nothing really worked. That's when the Society took shape, for the tranno Ghost Healers (as they called themselves) understood that these manufactured machines were not robots at all. They were the elementary particles of desire.

A True Story of the Past

As I write this I am 108 years old. I do this now because 108 is a special number, 1/240th of the Great Year, the time it takes for the constellations to make a complete rotation around the earth. But hey, who's counting? Apparently, only us Ancient Ones, the refugees from the Old World who managed to sail across the Nano Sea into the land of forever. We came to consciousness in a different world, marked by life spans and decay, birthdays and fixed identities. My lover, Callisto, a bright singer in nano-paradiso, likes me to tell her stories of those days. She says it reminds her that everything, including the nannies who release us from form and limitation, all come from the dust of dead stars. So here is something that happened long ago, in the year 1972, Old Calendar.

I was living in London back then, a baby pre-op (as we used to say in those days of scalpels and drugs), and my girlfriend and I held a trans central station open house on Tuesday nights. For a while a Japanese woman named Reiko was one of our regular visitors. Truth is, Reiko wasn't really her name, I don't remember her name, it was so long ago. Reiko is the name of a friend of mine who gave me permission to transplant her name into my memory.

Truth is, Reiko wasn't really a woman, at least not by the rigid standards of 1972. She was a Japanese businessman assigned to a dreary job in a London office. But when she came to us, she was beautiful. And I don't mean just in our sympathetic, loving trannie eyes. I don't know what Reiko looked like as a man, but as a woman she was tall, austere, and stunning, even by the rigid standards of 1972.

One evening she left her drab businessman body at home and stepped out as Reiko. I imagine her walking in Mayfair, or Bond Street, both graceful and nervous, her movements more elated with every step. At a certain point she stopped before a store window, maybe to look at a sapphire necklace or something as simple as a purple shawl.

She was standing there when she heard people talking in Japanese about a beautiful woman. They were admiring the woman's dress, her hair, her bearing. Quietly, Reiko glanced around to see who it was, and discovered that there was no one else, they were talking about her. What they said thrilled her, except—they were speaking in her own language. They were standing a few feet away from her and talking about her as if they could not imagine she would understand a word they were saying. Suddenly she realized. *They did not know she was Japanese.*

She was tall, taller than most Japanese men, in her high heels impossibly tall for a Japanese woman. Or maybe they saw she was trans, and while they admired the style and performance they could not imagine that a Japanese man, whether executive or salaryman, would ever do such a thing. Standing before that shop window, bathed in the thrill of her true self, Reiko had lost her nationality, her language. She'd become an exile from a people who could not comprehend the possibility of her existence.

A True Story of the Future

Callisto saw her first High Trans when she was young enough that she'd just undergone her third round of nano-vaccination. Five or six, I would guess. She herself just shrugs her soft wide shoulders like pillars of air and says she doesn't remember her age. Oh, but she remembers every detail of that first glimpse of the Living World.

From Callisto's description it must have been Katrina Harp, one of the five original Ghost Healers who founded the Nanochine Society. She remembers that the woman—man—creature—floated a little off the ground. Probably what she was seeing were the visible traces of the nano cloud that swirls all about a High T. Callisto had been out walking with her mother, who may or may not have suspected that her sweet boy was infected with the Germ of Becoming, as someone once called whatever it is that makes us trans. If Mom did know, she probably suppressed the thought—even now, mothers still want to believe their children are normal—but she must have worried about something because she tried to keep little C. from looking. No chance. That five-year-old probably would have wrestled Mom to the ground if it was the only way to view that wondrous sight.

Harp, if that in fact is who she saw, was very tall, with gentle breasts and hips softened by a sheen of water that flowed up and down her body. Her long hair moved constantly, changing not just color but form, sometimes a stream of bright particles, sometimes waves of light. She was wearing a ragged dress of many colors, probably nano-silk, while up and down the arms long wavery strands of light emerged directly from her nearly black skin. And there was writing on her. Words and symbols in unknown alphabets, diagrams and drawings, they were written directly on her skin in yellow, blue, and lavender. She looked, Callisto said, like a treasure map to another universe. Which, of course, is what she was.

Harp bent down to face her. She was so tall, Callisto said, her knees looked like mountains, her face like the sun rising between them. "Don't be afraid," Harp said. "You and I, we dream the world."

"No," Callisto's mother said, but without much conviction. But when Harp opened her mouth to breathe on the child, and Mom saw the famous perfumed cloud, she grabbed her darling boy-child and ran off down the street as fast as she could wobble with a five-year-old pressed to her chest and belly.

"Poor Mommy," Callisto said to me once, as she rolled herself tighter into my arms. "I was struggling so hard to get down, or just to see, I'm surprised we didn't both collapse in the street."

"She should have let you," I said. "She was only delaying what had to happen."

"But she didn't know that, did she? She was just trying to protect me."

"You? Or herself?"

She shrugged, and the way we fit together it shivered sweetly through my body. "I don't know," she said. "Maybe in her mind they were the same."

Two days later Callisto was missing. Her parents ran up and down the streets, with her father convinced that "that creature" had kidnapped their child. It was laughable, really. If Harp had wanted the child, she could have just sent a government team to adopt her. But why? We don't recruit. If you're not born a T cell in the body of God no nano sex change will make a difference. And it's not as if we're dying out. The fact is, many parents, either poor or just ambitious, dress their children in whatever they think looks trans in hopes they can propel the kid into the ranks of the people who rule their world. We send them home.

Callisto's parents finally found their baby at the edge of a river that ran past the housing complex a couple of miles from Callisto's home. Callisto had stolen one of her sister's dresses, a ruffly thing in white, and used the baby pocket knife Daddy had given her (she still has it, sometimes wears it on a gold chain around her neck) to slash it into tatters. She'd taken one of Mom's scarves as well, and cut streamers from it to tie on her arms and legs, and with a couple of crayons had written meaningless signs and pretend formulas in some imaginary language up and down her body.

She didn't hear her parents at first. She was staring at the water, imagining the river was her, and she was swept away, formless and bright, into an ocean of mystery at the end of the world.

Her mother screamed and ran up to grab her, though I'm sure she knew it was too late, it had always been too late.

Callisto turned and spoke calmly, but not in any human language. "It was all squeaks and clicks," she said to me. "I didn't really have any idea what it was supposed to mean. I just thought it was what I'd seen written on her body."

Her mother started crying, but her father, a man of action, hit her across the face. Hearing this, I let my Old World instincts take over, and I assumed her father was "queerphobic," or whatever quaint term we used before genuine civilization came into the world. But no. He was a man of his time, after all. What he yelled was "You think you're better than us? Gonna leave us behind and laugh at us? Gonna become one of *them*? You think creatures like that, with all their money and their nanomachine factories, you think they care about people like us?"

Callisto ran away five times growing up. It wasn't to escape her parents. After that first time they were more than a little afraid of her, and not very likely to harm her. And if they tried she had learned from a trans boy in school that she could report them to the Transgeneration Child Protection Agency. No, my little Callisto wasn't really running *away*. She was looking for people with writing on their bodies.

Over the years she found a few, including a lover, Hermes Tree, whose penis was so cleverly inscribed it displayed Orphic love poetry when collapsed, but when it opened up those same markings became part of detailed alchemical diagrams, what Hermes Tree called "the nano codes of creation." But she never found Harp again. Truth is, no one has seen Harp for thirty years. People claim to have sensed her, to feel her all around them, but her body seems to have freed itself from a fixed reality altogether.

When Callisto first transformed she spent the entire seclusion time after the insertion talking to her nannies in that same made-up language in which she'd answered her mother years before. She'd decided not to write it out on the surface. It was only for her and "the children," as she called the microscopic tribe that created her and still lives inside her. But sometimes, when we make love, I can see the messages come awake under her skin, I can hear the nannies in her blood whistling and clicking to each other.

Sometimes afterwards, as our dissolved bodies come back together, Callisto will ask me for a story. "Tell me of the Old World," she said to me once. "Tell me how it changed, what it felt like."

"Okay," I said, "but I won't do it directly. Let me make a fairy tale out of it."

"Ah," she said, and smiled up at me with a face bright shining as the Sun.

The Beatrix Gates

Once upon a time there was a girl named Kara, who lived in the Tribe of Red. Red people only ate food of that color, just as the Tribe of Green only ate green food. People were just made that way. Their bodies were different, their skins varied shades of their tribe, their hands and faces different, their inner organs even formed differently. The good thing was that the Reds desired exactly their own kind of food and the Greens desired theirs. They lived in different parts of town, with Green or Red restaurants and shops, and everyone was happy.

Except for Kara. From as early as she could remember she wanted to eat green food. And more, she wanted to wear Green-styled clothes, which were not all green, but shared certain styles and shapes and fabrics, and were cut to fit green bodies. Sometimes she worried that she wanted to leave her tribe altogether and become a Green. But that was impossible. God clearly had made her Red, and that was who she was. Yet—sometimes—if she was really honest with herself, if she felt deep inside to what was true, she didn't just *want* to be a Green, she believed, insanely, that she actually was.

It made no sense. She was not stupid or crazy, she could see herself in the mirror, a normal Red. Greens had a ridge over the eyebrows, lines on the sides of the neck, long fingers, a separated upper lip. Kara had none of that. She hated her flat forehead, her stubby fingers, but she knew they were there. But if she closed her eyes, and stood in the center of her bedroom, and said, "I am Kara, of the Tribe of Green," then her body opened up, and all her cells smiled. If she tried to take herself firmly in hand, and say "Don't be ridiculous. You know you're Red, you just need to grow up and accept it," her skin tightened, and her cells shrank in on themselves, and her lungs wept and refused to take in any more air.

As a teenager, the desire for everything Green, but especially Green food, became overwhelming. When she couldn't stand it, she would go behind a Green restaurant or grocery and look for scraps of thrown away food that she ate so fast she came close to choking. This was dangerous, for if someone discovered her she would be arrested and ridiculed, maybe even beaten or put in a mental hospital. And even though it felt so good while she did it, afterwards she would lie in bed, hugging her shame and silently crying with the light off, lest her mother come ask what was wrong. Her mother loved her and wanted the best for her, but the best would mean some kind of treatment to make her normal. How her father would react she didn't want to think about.

Much more satisfying were the rare moments she could disguise herself as a Green and go out in the world, maybe even buy a meal in a Green fast food restaurant, one without a long line where people might have time to examine her closely. It wasn't easy. She needed to buy—or steal—Green clothing, along with devices and makeup to change the shape of her body. Even more difficult was finding a place to put it all on. Greens and Red did mix in certain places, such as theaters or large department stores, but it was very dangerous to walk into a ladies' room as a Red and emerge as a Green. If she were caught, they'd lock her up as a dangerous pervert.

Could she really eat green food, or was she just fooling herself? It didn't make her throw up as every Red had always said it would (a girl at school had said, "If I even think of green food I get nauseous," and everyone agreed, even Kara, so no one would suspect her). But her body couldn't really digest it. When she was a child she would pray every night to the Red God to let her go, and the Green God to change her so she could eat her "real" food, as she thought of it. Every morning, when she woke up and examined herself and discovered she was still Red, with Red clothes in the closet, and a Red mother who set out a bowl of berries for her, and a Red father who crunched red cereal in his thick red teeth, she prayed silently, "If you won't change me, kill me. Please kill me." As she got older she stopped the prayers but not the desire to die.

One day a new teacher, a Red of course, came to teach science in Kara's high school. He looked like everyone else but there was an air about him, a kind of secret delight. Kara had to control herself from staring and staring. Finally, she deliberately messed up an exam so she could request a meeting to discuss her grade.

As soon as she was in the deserted classroom with him she closed the door, strode up to stand over him at his desk, and said, "You did it. You changed."

He got up to walk past her to open the door. "I have no idea what you're talking about."

She closed the door again. "You crossed over."

"Stop that," he said, and once more opened the door. "You want me to lose my job?"

"I'm sorry," she said, and then softly, "but I have to know how you did it. You were a Green and now you're a Red. *Please.*"

He tried to summon up a denial, to mold his face into a what-are-you-crazy, but it fell apart in a burst of compassion. Instead he just looked at her, and with a sigh he walked over and shut the door.

He knew what she wanted, he told her. He'd known from the first day he'd seen her, and dreaded this moment, for it was a hard life, and even though it had its own beauty, no one could understand it. The best you could hope for was that you change and no one ever know. Worst of all, he said, was that it really wasn't anything you could choose. The desire, the need, was so strong it was like . . . He frowned.

Kara said, "Like being whipped by God."

His eyes widened, and then he smiled. "Yes."

"How?" she demanded. "How did you do it?"

He told her of a group of alchemical doctors hidden in a far desert, people who'd studied the essence of Green and Red, and ways to change bodies through herbs, scalpels, and even spirits so subtle they could enter the body through small cuts on the palms or directly through the breath. To find these people she would have to travel through many lands and across dangerous territory. There was one thing that would help her. In every place there were people like them. Some, like the teacher himself, had made the journey and returned, others were weak, either physically or emotionally, but they loved the ones who could do it, and helped them in any way they could. That way they might imagine they themselves were passing through the "Alchemist's Palace," finally able to eat the food they had craved all their lives. Together, all these people formed what they called the Underground Caravan to help the Changers on their way.

Kara didn't dare tell her parents what she was going to do. They would try to stop her, and if she got away, and succeeded, she would come back a Green, unable to live in their world of Redness ever again. She left them a letter to ask their forgiveness, saying only that she had to do the most important thing in her life and they would never see her again. With what little money she had, and the address of the nearest stop on the Underground Caravan, that tunnel through the world, she set out.

She traveled for two years, the hardest, but also the most exciting time of her life. Even if she could have gone there directly it was very far away, but the path of help zigzagged so much she felt like a ball of dust blown from one corner of a room to another. When she ran out of money she discovered there were men who would pay her to wear green clothes and eat green food until she vomited on herself. She hated them and sometimes imagined killing them even as she smiled and made loud smacking noises with her lips as she took a bite.

Finally she saw it. Kara had expected something grand and ancient, with stone turrets or golden domes. Instead, she came over a hill of cracked brown dirt, with a green scarf wound around her face to protect her from what she thought of as red winds, and saw a low building of stone and glass. It looked like it had grown out of the desert floor. Over the stone, green and red vines twined together. Looking at them Kara felt both queasy and excited.

Before she approached the building she reached into her bag for a green cloak. She'd stolen it years ago from an unlocked house and kept it hidden under a pile of old toys in her parents' garage. Now she'd carried it on her journey and sometimes wrapped it around her when she slept, if she thought no one would spot her. She swirled it around her and fastened the clasp.

Kara didn't know what she expected. Maybe a kindly doctor would step out, or a group of Changed Greens who would welcome her with a platter of delicacies. Instead, a door opened and a tiger and leopard slinked out, each step slow and deliberate, as if they wanted to make clear there was no need to rush. The black eyes fixed on her, the teeth gave off sparks in the sun. Instead of yellow and black the tiger was red with green stripes, the leopard green with blood-red spots.

Kara backed away. She looked all around, as if someone might rush up and rescue her. No one. "Please," she said, not sure if she talked to the beasts or to someone hidden in the building. "It's not fair. I've come all the way across the world. I gave up everything."

"Not everything," the tiger said, and moved low to the ground, tensed to jump.

The cloak, she thought. They were punishing her for wearing a green cloak when she was still a Red. It was so unfair, they were supposed to be different, to help. Backing away, she reached up to the clasp. If she took it off, would they let her go? Maybe she could throw it at their heads so they couldn't see as she ran back over the hill.

No, she thought, with the clasp half-open. She'd rather die for real that run back to a dead life. She re-fastened the cloak and stepped forward. The tiger and leopard leaped at her throat.

Over the next weeks Kara knew consciousness at only rare moments. There was pain, and stabs of pleasure, and tiny bursts of light that went off under her skin. Ghosts moved alongside her, Green and Red nurses and doctors. Sometimes she saw an old woman with loose silver hair, a long white dress, and skin so smooth and colorless it seemed almost transparent. Kara had never seen someone who was neither Red nor Green, and she would have stared if she'd not been too tired to keep her eyes open. The woman said her name was Beatrix. When she stroked Kara's forehead with the tips of her fingers green light ran through Kara's body.

Kara woke up for real in a green wooden bed, under a green cover. She realized she was wearing a green nightdress, while alongside the bed a green robe lay over a wooden chair painted all over with green vines. Ignoring the wobbliness in her legs, Kara jumped up and ran to a mirror on the side wall. Yes! She could see the change in her face and skin. She was Green! And hungry, unequivocally hungry, with no more horrible choice of eating food she hated or food her body could not really accept.

Just then a man came in, a young Red with a silver tray of food, all of it green, green, green. He laughed happily at her greedy appetite, her sighs of delight. It sounded like the laughter of someone who knew just how it felt. It struck Kara—she'd never thought this before—that as much as she was Green, and had always been Green, she was something else as well. She belonged to a secret tribe, the Changers. Her bond with this transformed Red, this man she didn't know and could never be close to in the outside world, might be stronger than with any Green she would ever meet. She thought of all the Greens and Reds who'd helped her find her way to the Alchemist's Palace. She reached over to hug the young nurse. What would outsiders think of *that*? A Green hugging a Red. They both laughed.

She sat down on the chair. "Is Beatrix here?"

Nurse Red stared at her. "Beatrix?" he said softly. "You saw her?"

"Yes, of course," Kara said. "She helped me when I was hurting."

"Just a moment." He got up and left the room. A few minutes later he came back with a short elderly man, a dark-skinned Green in an elegant white suit. "Good morning," he said. "I am Dr. Virgilian."

"Oh," she said. "Were you the one—Did you change me?"

"Yes. Many of us worked on you, but I led them."

"Thank you! Thank you so much!"

"Rosso tells me you were visited by a woman named Beatrix. Would you mind telling me what she looked like?"

"Of course," Kara said. She described the old woman, and added, "I assumed she worked here."

"Not exactly," Dr. Virgilian said. "She shows up from time to time. On a volunteer basis."

"Oh. Well if you see her could you tell her I want to thank her? She was really very nice to me."

"Yes, certainly. Tell me something, Kara. Are you happy? Now that you've changed."

"Oh yes. This is all I've ever wanted. Thank you so much."

Dr. Virgilian smiled. "Then we are happy as well. Congratulations, Kara. Welcome to your new life." He clasped both her hands in his for a moment, then bowed slightly before he walked to the door. With his hand on the knob he turned and said, "Feel free to explore the building and the grounds. And if I don't see you again before you return to the world, please remember that you are always welcome here."

"Thank you," she said.

"Oh, by the way," he added, "the name Beatrix? It means 'she who brings happiness.' I looked it up once. Isn't that interesting?"

Kara stayed for over a week. She watched the Alchemists in their laboratories whose walls were covered with symbols and formulas. She talked with other "transcolorists," a term she learned from Rosso, who himself had come years ago, expecting to change and leave but had decided there was no place he would rather be.

One afternoon she was sitting in a sun room with a young man named Willem, a New Green like Kara herself. Kara asked, "Were you scared out of your mind when that tiger and leopard came out?"

Willem squinted at her. "What?"

Kara wanted to run from the room. She said, "You know, when you first came to the Palace."

"I don't know what you mean. I knocked on the door and Rosso opened it and welcomed me. I was very happy I did not have to explain anything."

"Oh," Kara said. She felt herself shiver, and hugged herself. "I've got to go." All that day she wanted to ask Rosso or even

Dr. Virgilian but didn't want them to think she was crazy. She must have passed out from hunger and dreamed it all.

The night before she was due to return to the world Green Kara woke up to a strange sound. A mix of sustained high-pitched notes and low, sharply punctuated cries, it seemed a kind of singing, but nothing she'd ever heard or imagined. She was not even sure if it was human.

She put on her green robe and stepped into the empty corridor. Where was everybody? Couldn't they hear it? She walked towards the sounds. After various turns down different passages she came to a spiral staircase she'd never seen before. She squinted up at it, confused, for it seemed to reach higher than she remembered the height of the building. It was dark, but at the very top she could see points of color and a shimmering line of white. Beatrix?

Kara climbed for a long time. With every turn the singing (if that was what it was) became louder, the high notes piercing her skin, the low a shock to her bones. A couple of times she tripped and almost rolled down again but managed to stop herself so she could push upwards.

The first thing she saw when she reached the top was the open gates. There were two doors, one green, the other red, both engraved with complex diagrams that looked like messages. On the other side of the opening she saw first nothing but darkness and tiny lights that appeared and disappeared, with swirling lines that seemed to vanish in on themselves.

As she continued to stare she thought she saw the tiger and leopard, fighting or dancing with each other, so fast she could hardly see them. And there were people, or at least she thought there were, so hard to see. Maybe it was just a trick of the lights, for now she could see color and pattern, green and red, and colors Kara's eyes couldn't even figure out. She stared, her mouth open, her fists clenched.

It took a few moments before she saw Beatrix on the left side of the gates. Her white dress shone dimly in the dark. She said, "Beloved Kara. The Gates are open for you. You may enter or leave. There is no blame."

Kara lifted a foot. If she passed through she would become something she couldn't even imagine. She would know rushes of color and tone most people never suspected. Except—she would have to give up her life as a Green. There were no Greens or Reds beyond the gates, only color that never ended and never stayed the same. "I'm sorry," she said to Beatrix. "I waited so long. I'm sorry." She turned and ran, as fast as she could, down to the solid ground of the Alchemist's Palace.

The trip back to the world was much easier than the journey out. Rosso gave her money and maps, and now that she was a proper Green she could eat, and be with her own people, whenever she wanted. She found a town she liked, and got a job, and went back to school, and eventually became a librarian. She made friends, even fell in love a couple of times, though never for very long. How could she tell a lover the most important thing about her? It was only late at night that she sometimes wondered, just what *was* that thing? That she had been a Red and was now a Green? Or that she passed up the chance to become something else?

She joined the transcolor underground network, sheltering travelers and directing them to the next stop. She helped so many they called her "the Travel Agent." She found small groups of neo-Greens, and even a mixed group of Greens and Reds. It thrilled her to discover how much their lives were like hers, the childhood of loneliness and fear, the desire that made you feel like a leaf in a hurricane of fire. And then the discovery of hope, the ecstasy of change. But she never mentioned the tiger and leopard, or the singing, or the doorway she thought of as the Beatrix Gates.

After fifteen years had gone by, Kara traveled back to her hometown. For a week she stayed in a Green hotel, went to all the Green restaurants, and the Green markets. She watched groups of teenaged Green girls, or Green children in their Green playground. Finally she took a taxi to her parents' home and rang the bell.

Kara's mother answered the door. Her face sagged a little, and she looked shorter, but she was dressed more carefully than Kara remembered, in a red skirt and jacket that looked almost elegant. Distaste flickered in her face before she coated it with politeness. It was nothing personal, Kara knew, just what any Red feels towards a Green who shows up on her doorstep. Kara had felt the same way once, when a Red plumber came to fix her toilet.

"Can I help you?" Kara's mother said.

"Mom," Kara said, "it's me. Kara."

"What?"

"I've changed, Mom. I always wanted to change and I did it. That was why I left. But it's me. I missed you."

"How dare you?" her mother said. "I don't know who you think you are or who sent you with that sick joke."

"It's not a joke. I'm your daughter."

"My daughter was Red. Can't you see that? What's the matter with you? She was a beautiful Red girl and she disappeared a long time ago. Some Green pervert must have taken her. If you don't get out of here right now I'm calling the police."

"Mom, please—" Kara's mother slammed the door. Kara walked away.

Years passed. Kara became head of the regional library system, where she promoted books on openness and tolerance. She continued her work with the Underground Caravan, and even received an award at a secret convention deep in the mountains. She hid the plaque—gold, with green and red swirls that reminded her of the Palace—in the bottom drawer of her night table.

One evening, at a Green health club, she met a schoolteacher named Devra, who was bright and funny.

They went for a drink, and then the next night dinner, and soon they were lovers. Devra was wonderful and Kara even thought she loved her. But after some months Devra wanted marriage, and while Kara thought this would be wonderful and could even imagine them as old women together in a house by the sea, she knew she could not get married without telling Devra her secret. She broke it off. For some time she berated herself for cowardice and a too-long habit of secrecy. Then one night, as she was sitting alone with a glass of green curaçao, it struck her that she wouldn't know what to say. In the years before she'd changed she would have known exactly what to say, the same narrative she now heard over and over from the people she helped. Something shifted, however, that last night in the Palace. It left her with a riddle that seemed beyond solution.

As time went on, a new spirit of openness stirred in Kara's country. People talked about Greens and Reds becoming friends, even lovers, though many wondered how this could happen since sharing food was so important in romance, and they'd get sick if they even cooked together.

One Sunday morning Kara sat down with a cup of green tea and the paper. Suddenly she gave a cry and spilled her tea. The magazine cover showed a handsome adolescent Green staring out at the camera. The lighting allowed his face to shine while hiding his clothes. You could see the eyebrow ridge, the separated lip, the lines in the neck that clearly marked him a

Green. Across the bottom of the page, in bright pink, were the words "I AM A RED!"

Kara read the article three times and might have read it forever if the phone calls hadn't started. Everything was there, the longing, the hopelessness, the constant thoughts of suicide. There were various attempts at explanations, talk of nature's (or God's) mistakes, fetal brain chemistry, and so on, none of which interested Kara in the slightest. More important was the claim that the "condition," while very rare, occurred in Greens and Reds of every culture.

Would people suspect her, Kara wondered. Her best guess was no, though her hands shook even as she pretended to think calmly. She'd been Green for so long, was so established, looked just like any other middle-aged Green woman.

Some of the callers worried about their own safety. Others hoped the outside world would become more tolerant. Still others worried if the Caravan would have to increase security, and what it all might mean to the Alchemist's Palace. After several hours Kara stopped answering the phone.

She went and lay down on her bed, stared up at the pale-green ceiling. What did it all mean? If it all became public, maybe even accepted, would that make it normal? Or understood? Did she herself understand anything?

To Kara's relief no great change happened. People discussed the article with fascination or disgust. Some made jokes about it, or claimed it was all a hoax. Kara took a tolerant stand admired by many of her friends. Soon the question was mostly forgotten.

One day, thirty-two years after she'd left the red and green building in the desert, Kara saw a sign outside a planetarium. "Music of the Spheres," it read. "Ancient dream, modern reality?" She was in a city new to her, for a conference, and had the afternoon free, so she stepped inside.

The planetarium was a circular room with a dome-like ceiling and wide seats that tilted back like dentist's chairs. Though there was no official separation, custom gave the left side to Greens, the right to Reds. Kara sat down among a class of chattering high school students. There was more space on the right, but you just didn't do that. She would have been uncomfortable, even if no one else was sitting there.

The room went dark and the ceiling lit up with an old-fashioned image of the heavens, a blue-black sky with the constellations marked in dotted lines. A recorded man's voice intoned platitudes about the ancients' belief in gods and spirits. The image shifted to concentric circles with the earth in the center and small circles labeled with the names of the sun, moon, and planets. The speaker told how people believed that the earth was at the center of a series of spheres, each one with its own musical tone corresponding to the diatonic scale. Sonorous sounds echoed around the room.

Sadly, the voice said, this vision of harmony ended (sudden silence) when people discovered that the universe was vastly greater than the solar system, with the earth a speck at the edge of a mundane galaxy. Now the image shifted to swirls of color, red and green, but also blue, yellow, purple, all rushing away and replaced by new explosions of light.

Has the music ended, the voice asked, and answered itself no. A different kind of music has emerged, more subtle and far stranger. A deep hum sounded—the background radiation of the Big Bang, the voice explained. Higher electronic notes followed, a supposed version of the radio waves given off by stars and far away galaxies, followed by staccato sounds that represented pulsars. The universe sings to us all the time, the voice proclaimed. We are not equipped to hear it but we know it is there.

No, Kara thought. We can hear it. We have to open ourselves, not just our ears but our whole bodies. We have to become something . . . no longer human? No longer Red or Green, or any fixed color at all. But the singing, the voices, the *invitation*, is always there. It never stops, ever.

She was shaking now. The teenage girl next to her edged away, whispered to her friend who looked over at Kara and giggled. Kara didn't care. She knew at last what she'd heard that night at the Palace. It was the universe itself, singing to her. The people she saw were the ones who had gone through, and they all sang to her through the deep longing in the curve of space, the passionate love that spiraled through galaxies. And they didn't just sing of the vast cosmos. Her own cells, the mighty civilizations of molecules and atoms that made up her body, the leptons and baryons and all the patterns between them, they were all held together by music, the song of songs of desire.

She had to leave. She stood up, ignored the grunts and whispers of the teenagers. With just the slightest shift she could pass right through their bodies. Like her, all they were was music.

She rushed out of the building, stood among the trees outside the museum. She closed her eyes and realized she didn't know if the trees were red or green. She held her arms out slightly from her body, the hands opened, the fingers pointed at the ground. She realized now. *She'd never stopped hearing it.* She could hear it right now, she'd been hearing it for thirty-two years. She'd only pretended to herself that it ended when she ran down the stairs. It never ended, she heard it in her fingers, in the breath of everyone around her, in the leaves, the trash in the street, the dirt, the electrons that surged through the concrete.

And something more. She was still there. Still at the top of the staircase, still staring through the Beatrix Gates. She'd never left.

Oh, she knew very well that her body, middle-aged and green, stood upright on a street, outside a building of steel and concrete and glass. This was real, and the cars were real, and the pigeons (she could hear the clumsy flap of their wings), the shoppers and commuters, the automatic doors that hissed open and closed. It was all real. But so were the Gates at the top of the stairs. In every moment, whatever she did—drinking green coffee at her desk, talking on the phone to another helper from the Caravan, making precious Green love to Devra (did that too go on forever and ever?), crying outside her mother's red door, half-asleep in her bathtub after a long workday, praying for death when she was nine years old—at every moment she *also* stood, shaking and frightened and newly Green, at the top of a spiral, before a woman who was old and young and colorless and every color at once, and beyond her the forever open Gates.

Could she will herself there? Right now? Vanish from the street and reappear at the doorway? Eyes still closed, she drew her body into herself, arms across her chest, feet together, chin down. She tried to let the music fill her, expand her, make her a pulse of sound. No. The songs were real, and the Gates, and Beatrix, serene and patient, but so were the buses and the museum building and the couple arguing down the street. She laughed and opened her eyes. All right then, she would do it the old-fashioned way.

She set off down the street towards the garage with her little green car in it, and with every step the universe surged alongside her. A block before the garage entrance she saw a Green boy, about seven, crouched down in a doorway. He was playing intensely with a two-inch-high action figure. "Captain

Red," it was called. Kara'd seen it once on TV. Every few seconds the boy's eyes flicked up, then back to his toy. Heaven pulsed in his chest.

Kara bent down in front of him, watched him cringe and hide the toy in his pocket. She knew it was the most precious thing he'd ever owned. "It's all right," she told him. "You're a good boy." She wanted to say, "The sky loves you," but he wouldn't understand. Very carefully she said, "When I was your age, I was Red."

He stared at the ridge over her eyes, the rich green of her face and hands. "Yes," she said, "it's true. You can change. It can happen." Now she got out a pen and a scrap of paper from her purse and in green ink wrote down a phone number. "Hide this somewhere," she said as she gave it to him. "And memorize the number in case you can't keep it. When you're ready call them and say that Kara the Travel Agent wants them to guide you. Do you understand?" He nodded. Kara said, "You need to say it."

He whispered, "Yes."

Kara smiled and gently kissed the top of his head. Galaxies swirled under his scalp. "We have been here forever," she said.

Kara's second journey to the Alchemist's Palace took less than a quarter of the time for the first. She knew the way, and she had a car, and people to help her. She arrived on a chilly winter afternoon, with the faded old cloak—she'd saved it all these years—once more wrapped around her.

The tiger and the leopard were waiting outside the building before she arrived. She stood before them, arms up and welcoming. "I'm ready," she said. But instead of mauling her, they just rubbed her legs like kittens, then urged her around the corner to a yellow door she'd never seen before. When she opened the door, there it was: the spiral staircase.

All along the journey she had imagined herself running up the stairs, lifted by the music and her own joy. Now she moved very slowly, each step deliberate, for she wanted the entire experience. She first saw Beatrix about halfway up. The spiral turned her towards and away and she would twist her head to try to keep the woman in sight, as if she might vanish, and the singing stop, the moment Kara lost sight of her.

When she reached the Gates they looked duller than she remembered. There were no flashes of light or sudden flares of color, no mysterious figures waiting for her, and she panicked that she might have made a mistake. It was the music that sustained her. It thrilled her, vibrated her veins and stretched her skin, so that she thought she might break apart at any moment.

Then she realized why the Gates seemed dull, or empty. She was staring at colors she'd never known existed. There were tones and brightnesses for which she had no words, and so her mind had tried not to see them. She closed her eyes, opened them, and waves of color swamped her. She could see people in them, and animals and landscapes, all of it shimmers of impossible color.

At the top she took Beatrix's hands, so thin and translucent. "I'm sorry," she said. "For staying away so long."

"I was always with you," Beatrix said.

"Are you coming now? Through the Gates?"

Beatrix shook her head, and for a moment the silver hair became all those colors beyond color. Then it was once more ancient silver, as Beatrix said, "You are not the last."

Kara leaned forward and kissed Beatrix on the lips. Suddenly she discovered she was on the other side. *The Gates are my own body*, she thought. She was here, and Green, and Red, and every color possible and not possible, surrounded by lovers and worlds as strange and wondrous as Kara herself.

She was every color, and she was nothing, nothing at all. Nothing singing. Nothing filled with the music of everything.

Could she have gone to this place without all the struggle to change her color? If Green and Red were so limited, couldn't she just have jumped past them? No. She knew the answer immediately. She had to become who she really was before she could become nothing. The key that opened the Beatrix Gates was passion.

And with that understanding, once upon a time ended, and she lived happily ever after, forever and never.

Something That Happened Long Ago

For two years in the last century before the world changed, I wrote a comic book. It was called *Doom Patrol*, and it told of a group of superheroes who all had terrible problems with their bodies. There was a head with no body at all, and a robot with a human brain, and a couple who were pure energy contained in bandages to give them a physical form, and a girl who was so ugly no one had ever loved her so that she created imaginary friends, each with its own super-power. Into this mix I introduced Kate Godwin, a.k.a. Coagula, a transsexual lesbian superhero. Kate could dissolve and coagulate any form of matter (the result of sex with an alchemist) but her real super-power was much simpler. She accepted herself. She became the team's emotional leader, guiding them through various close calls with the end of the world (the book was prophetic) because she trusted desire.

After several months of Kate's stories, a letter came to us from a reader in England. She called herself M.A. She wrote, "You have given me the courage to realize I do not have to feel ashamed of who I really am." And, "For as long as I can remember I have been miserable and only carried on living because I was too afraid that death would hurt too much. I did not realize that I was dead all the time. When I was a child I would pray to God every night that when I woke up in the morning I would have changed, of course I never did." And,

"Thanks to the message you have conveyed using 'Kate,' and the support I have gotten from friends since I told them, I now feel that I can do something about my situation, that before I never really perceived I could alter."

Several years later, I went to a movie called *A.I.* in which a woman rejects her android son. Imprinted with love for his mother forever, the android remembers the story *Pinocchio*, in which a Blue Fairy changes a puppet to a real boy. The android boy thinks how if he became real then his mother would love him. He travels across the country until he finds a statue of a woman in a sunken amusement park. The woman is blue, and the android sits in front of it, underwater, for a thousand years, saying, over and over, "Please, Blue Fairy. Make me a real boy. Please, Blue Fairy. Make me a real boy. Please, Blue Fairy. Make me a real boy."

I sat in the movie theater, and I watched the child, knowing it didn't matter whether it was boy or girl, the prayer was to become real. And I thought to myself, *The Blue Fairy couldn't do it. God couldn't do it. I did it.*

The magic formula to make someone real is very simple. Trust their desire. Believe in passion.

This is a true story. It is all a true story, and a very old one.

Trans Central Station

Some words that did not exist when I transitioned	Some words that no longer (or almost no longer) exist
transition	sex change
transgender	transsexual
cisgender	transvestite
gender binary	real woman
gender nonbinary	real man
gender fluid	genuine girl (GG)
sex assigned at birth	genetic girl (GG)
gender assigned at birth	shemale
sex reassignment surgery (SRS)	he-she
gender reassignment surgery (GRS)	she-he
gender confirmation surgery (GCS)	female (or male) impersonator
trans woman	a woman trapped in a man's body
trans man	a man trapped in a woman's body

EACH OF THE LISTS above contains thirteen entries. Thirteen is the traditional number of a witch's coven, a place where spiritual outlaws perform magic, often in the service of—or maybe alignment with—the ancient Goddess of the moon, the hunt, mountains, and wild animals, especially bears, Artemis/Diana, a figure so old that no one actually knows the origin or meaning of the name "Artemis." We will return to Artemis—and bears—later in this essay.

When I was growing up, the idea that I should ever tell any-one of my desires—to wear girls' clothes and somehow, in some vague way, be thought of as girl—was unspeakable. I do not mean something vile, as in the old horror cliché, "an unspeakable evil," though there were people who might have thought that if I indeed had ever spoken of it. Nor did I mean something sinful, that which must not be spoken—though there certainly were people who would have thought, and said, *that*.

No. I mean something much more basic. What I felt, what I desired was unspeakable because, for me at least, the words did not exist. Or rather, the *telling* did not exist. Let me go further. To speak of such things, to anyone, was in fact, *un-thinkable*. The mind could not form the thought. I did not wish to tell people and didn't dare. I simply could not imagine doing it.

Let me be clear about something else. By "doing," I do not mean wear girls' clothes. I did *that*, with bits of my older sister's wardrobe, or even my mother's, when I had a reason-able certainty I would not get caught. No, I mean speaking, sharing, as the Twelve Step people say, with myself, God, and another human being. I certainly "spoke" with myself. I was very aware of my desires.

Oddly, I did not concern myself very much with God. I grew up in a Jewish family, members of an Orthodox *shul*, and considered myself religious until about fifteen, when I became an atheist. (Happily, that phase didn't last long—I now think of myself as "a radical, Goddess-loving Jew" or simply describe my religion as Heresy.) Somehow, it did not occur to me that God might consider my desires, and secret actions, as sinful or something to arouse "His" anger. Of course, nor did I expect God to approve. It simply seemed outside God's purview. Perhaps if I'd known about *Artemis*—but that came much later. I might add, however, that when that time came, and I had begun to explore the ancient roots of transgender, I came across places in the Torah that forbid both cross-dressing and castration. Oddly enough, I did not feel guilt, shame, or even anger. Rather, it excited me, because it meant people like me existed in Ancient Israel. You do not forbid what doesn't exist. But as I say, all that came later.

Growing up, I did not worry about God knowing my desires. But other *people*, even that proverbial "another human being," that lay beyond even imagination. This silence was not something that began, say, in adolescence. My earliest memory, from around four or five, involves that intense, conscious desire to wear girls' clothes, and that equally powerful, yet somehow mostly unconscious, conviction that absolutely no one must ever know. Not my parents, not some mythical best friend to whom I could tell *anything*—quite simply, no one.

People used to say of "transsexuals," by which they mostly meant transgender women, that they were "women trapped in men's bodies." (Some people attribute the expression, and the term "transsexual" itself, to a psychiatrist named Harry Benjamin, but I've seen that claim contested.) But that does not describe me.

When I came out, as a woman and a lesbian (this was 1971, and remember, the term "transition" did not exist then), I realized that I was in exactly the *right* body, for my body told me what it—what I—wanted. In the early '90s the activist Riki Wilchins came up with the wonderful slogan, "I'm not trapped in anybody's body." And Nor Hall, brilliant writer on mythology and the psyche, wrote once, "Abandonment to the body's desire is in itself a form of revelation."

No, I was not trapped in the wrong body. I was trapped in the wrong universe. In order to become who I was, I had to break the world open. I had to embrace a kind of science fiction life. Or maybe a magical life, by which I mean the ability to experience the world, and connections, and myself, in ways that did not fit the standard model of reality. I use that term, "standard model," ironically, for it refers to Niels Bohr's description of quantum physics as disconnected from the everyday world.

But of course I am not talking about "entangled particles," or quarks, or whether electrons are waves or particles, or even Schrödinger's long-suffering cat hidden inside a box and both alive and dead at the same time, until the famous "observer" opened the box and looked. Or maybe the cat is *exactly* the right metaphor, if we think of the box as the *closet*, and the experience of so many trans people—and queer people in general—as alive and dead at the same time, until they themselves open the box and allow the world to actually see them.

And even more—to see *ourselves*. For many trans people, this moment of seeing, of discovering that the cat is very much alive, comes as a kind of revelation. For me, it came in 1971. I had already taken small steps to open up. The radicalness of the times, especially the examples of women's liberation and the new gay liberation movement, encouraged me to tell my partner of my need to dress, secretly and only occasionally, as a woman.

To be fair, it was not so much the times as my own inner need simply getting worse when I thought it would get better. I married a wonderful woman named Edith Katz. This was not uncommon for people like me, who were in serious denial about how deep a part of our lives these needs were. We would sometimes convince ourselves that once in a "fixed" relationship all that "nonsense" would go away. And of course, it was indeed non-sense, a desire and yearning that made no sense, at least in the universe of fixed categories. So we would dismiss it, only to discover that the need intensified. I told Edie and experimented in very small ways, but things remained tense. Schrödinger's cat was not yet alive, but certainly not dead. To extend the metaphor, I had pried open the lid but had not dared to actually look.

And then came that moment. I was with some friends, just having fun, and at a certain point I was sitting by myself when the thought came that I could no longer put off *the question*. Did I want to become a woman? And almost the instant I allowed myself to ask that, the answer came like a kind of revelation. I did not *want* to be a woman. I already *was*.

Since then I've discovered other trans people's accounts of what I'm calling "the Moment." One woman said it was like a glass wall shattering. Her real life had always existed on the other side, and now she could enter it. Another said she had been going through great anxieties and told her girlfriend she was going to take a shower and try to clear her head. Standing in the water, she thought, "What's the worst this all could be?" A moment later she came out of the shower, dripping and astonished, and told her friend, "I'm a woman!" Her friend replied, "It's about time you figured that out."

A transman friend of mine once told me that for years, while he was trying to live as a woman, he would have a terrifying dream in which he would look into his grandmother's full-length mirror, the kind that turned on a hinge, with a second mirror on the other side. But when he looked, there was no one there, as if the person looking in the mirror did not really exist. When he finally accepted that he wasn't a butch lesbian, he was a man, he had the dream again. But now, as he stared at the empty glass, a voice said, "Turn me around." He flipped the mirror to the other side and saw a man staring back at him.

Consider a fantasy. A wizard casts a spell on a child, maybe before birth, so that she finds herself in a world that does not recognize the very possibility of her existence. The way out of this trap does not involve a counter-spell, or a discovery of the plot. Instead, it follows the path of desire, even when that desire seems incomprehensible.

Actually, Edith years ago came up with a lighthearted version of this fantasy. She suggested that my soul had decided to incarnate as a girl this time around, but a sorcerer had shunted me into a male body. My soul proved stronger than either the spell or the body's seemingly self-evident logic. Here is a possible title for a story: "The Illogical Body."

The physical world may be made out of elementary particles (and dark matter) but the world of our lives is made out of language. With the wrong language, one of strict categories and confinement, the world becomes a fake, a stage set whose actors don't know they are in a play, a Potemkin village whose inhabitants think they live in the real world. Most people do not notice this because their own sense of self, of language, more or less fits the received version of existence. They still suffer, for in a world of strict and very limited categories they must constantly check themselves against the model of a "real man" or a "real woman."

The ones who reveal the fake are the ones who simply cannot make themselves fit. To not fit can bring great pain, and often very real danger. Yet who else can discover the light behind the screen?

Let's look a moment at those dangers. There are, of course, the examples, far too many, of harassment, beatings, and murder. If those insane "bathroom laws" were ever put into effect, any or all of three things would happen to transwomen forced to use men's toilets: 1. rape, 2. beatings, 3. arrest on a charge of prostitution. And meanwhile, the very thing proponents of these laws claim to fear would happen—burly, bearded (trans) men using the women's room.

As well as physical and legal dangers, trans people, particularly young transmen and women, face a different kind of danger. This is identity loss, and it occurs through language. To call a transwoman "he" or a transman "she" is either a deliberate insult or something worse, a casual obliteration of the person's identity. Recently, young trans activists have come up with a powerful term for attacks on a person's very existence—dead-naming. Its fullest manifestation occurs when a young transperson dies, from disease sometimes, but more often through murder or suicide. The family, who may have thrown the adolescent out, now claim the body, dress it in the "original" gender, then hold a funeral and set up a tombstone, using only the name (and pronouns) the parents chose for the child. This is dead-naming. The person dies twice, first in the body, and then in memory, deliberately erased from existence.

By extension, any use of a person's old name to designate who they are is now called dead-naming, and people may refer to the name on their (original) birth certificate as their "dead name." Deliberately brutal, the expression shows trans people's passion in claiming their real, *alive* selves.

My first story was published under my old name (all other stories, articles, and books are under my "living," or chosen, name). This is a matter of public record. You can find it on the internet. But out of respect for all those people who struggle against dead-naming—and to be honest, my own struggle, when I first came out, to get people to respect my chosen name and pronoun—I choose not to use it.

Since so much of this account revolves around words—the way pronouns and terms like Mr. and Miss, and names, can imprison people, while claiming your true words can set you free—and since I am a writer, a "woman of words," to use the phrase of the great Mazatec shaman and poet María Sabinas, let us consider the prefix "trans."

There is, of course, "transparent," a term used in support groups well before the television show. But aside from its pun on parenting, think of what it means. To be clear, to allow the world to see you, all the way through.

And then, of course, there is "transgender" itself, and its antecedents, "transvestite" and "transsexual." I once met a man whom I privately dubbed "the happy cross-dresser." He loved dressing up privately, with his wife's enthusiastic support, but felt no need to go further. He told me a great story. He said that as a teenager he was filled with confusion, if not shame. Then he went, by himself, to see the movie *Psycho*. At the end, a psychiatrist says that Norman Bates, who dressed up as his mother to kill his victims, is not a transvestite. Now, Mark (not his real name, alive or dead) had taken some Latin in high school. Almost idly, he pondered the strange term. "Trans . . . cross. Vest . . . clothing . . . *There's a word for it!*" He ran out of the theater and headed for the nearest library.

Trans-port. To carry yourself from your assigned gender to a new one, or none at all. To be transported by ecstasy. And what port will you arrive at? Many people, including trans-people themselves at the start of their journey, may assume the port, the destination, is known—from woman to man, or man to woman, or either to none—only to discover, as they set off, that the wonder of the journey may open up the world to ports, destinations, never considered or even imagined. But perhaps I say this because I'm a science fiction writer. And maybe I'm a science fiction writer, at least in part, because I had no choice but to break open the world and discover what ports lay hidden behind its façade.

Trans-action. Not just the power of acting, of standing up for yourself, of simply *doing* something, but the transactions, the relationships between people that become possible when you take the action of letting them see who you really are.

And what of trans-mission? "Your mission, should you choose to accept it . . ." And yes, you must choose it, there is really no way around that, even if you know, as I do, that there really is no choice, except maybe death. Despite that, you must take the action. Come out. Tell people. Begin, finally, to live. Discover what world lies beyond the Potemkin façade of received categories.

Can you see why I was drawn to science fiction? And to comics? In the first, people were creating other worlds, worlds with different rules or structures. In the second, people changed their very selves, gaining "powers far beyond those of mortal men." When I came out and began to explore the world of trans possibilities (a very narrow world in the early '70s), I discovered something interesting. The small population of professional science fiction writers contained several people known to have "changed sex," as we used to say back then. And, judging from various writers' stories, there were others, from still earlier generations, who might have done it if the world had given them an opening.

Extending into the '80s, the number of trans people in the world was still just a handful. But back then, before the internet and online magazines, the entire population of professional science fiction writers was only a few thousand people. And according to the "official," that is, psychiatric statistics, the percentage of people in the general population was miniscule. I do not have the numbers on hand, but I seem to remember "one in ten thousand" being thrown about.

Now—well, Riki Wilchins, mentioned above, once commented that if it were easier to change sex, a lot more people would do it. It's astonishing how right she was. For my part, my second short story, "Tubs of Slaw" (the title came from a surreal comedy record by the Firesign Theatre) featured a group of children who receive their genitals from the government one afternoon and are disappointed to discover there are only two varieties. A little later, still in the '70s, I published "The Second Generation," in which people can take instant sex change pills that allow them to change back and forth between male and female all day long if they wished. This is their world, and the two young protagonists see nothing strange about it—until the day one of them, then the other, takes a pill—male or female, it doesn't matter—and changes into something entirely different, something completely unknown. The nano-tranno-paradiso of "The Beatrix Gates" is a kind of sequel to "The Second Generation."

Science fiction lures trans people with that possibility to imagine a different world. And the community of SF people, by and large, opened itself to trans people, gave us a chance to be ourselves.

In much of this essay it might seem as if I transitioned, heroically, all by myself. Nothing could be further from what happened. I did come to that life-changing realization that I was a woman—the shattering of the glass wall—essentially on my own. But Edith had been encouraging me to try to understand who I was. And when I did come out, she strongly supported me. I'm happy to say that this was not just altruism, or loyalty, some bizarre version of "stand by your man."

If anything, it was the opposite. She had become deeply involved in the women's liberation movement and preferred the idea of standing by her *woman*. (I could say vastly more about her, and her vital place in my life, but I prefer to respect her privacy.)

Women's liberation and then gay liberation helped open the world for me. They gave me models of how to trust your own experience rather than society's rules and stereotypes. When Edie and I moved to London in 1971 we joined GLF (the Gay Liberation Front) but also sought out trans groups. At first, I found this frustrating. I was looking for a political consciousness, a framework of ideas. The groups that existed seemed, well, light. And then I realized something. The liberation groups took everything very seriously, constantly arguing, theorizing. The trans groups liked to have *fun*. And that was when I understood that being trans was about joy almost more than anything else.

That did not mean I gave up on the idea of a group dedicated to raising consciousness. If one didn't exist, I would start it myself. Edith and I began to host weekly meetings in our flat in the Notting Hill section of London. My desire to discuss theory never got very far, but something important happened. We provided a place where people could be, and explore, themselves, at whatever level seemed comfortable. The Japanese transwoman described in the title story of this book was one of those people.

Another was a young and brilliant Oxford grad student, still in the closet in everyday life but excited to have a place to go and explore her secret self. Years later, Roz Kaveney has become an award-winning memoirist, poet, critic, activist, and yes, science fiction writer. A while back she wrote a short article about those days, in which she very kindly dubbed my London flat "trannie central."

Since then, and in fact since I used the word "trannie" in "The Beatrix Gates," the term has taken on some nasty meanings. Thinking of how I might change "trannie central," and being from New York and a lover of Grand Central Station, I came up with the title of this essay. "The Beatrix Gates" proved more problematic, since the utopian frame story plays on "trannie" and "nannie," the latter short for nano-machines. I kept one or two but changed the others. Hopefully, no young militants will take offense.

My activism comes and goes. Edith and I left London for Amsterdam in 1973 and while I stayed connected to trans people I focused on my writing and enjoying life. Partly my step back from political action came from the trauma of discovering that the women's movement, especially the more radical branches of it, where I'd felt a natural home, wanted nothing to do with me. They saw me, and people like me, as something akin to creations of mad scientists (I am not exaggerating, believe me). Over time I came to see their hostility as a kind of secret blessing. If they had welcomed me, I might have adopted their views for the sake of fitting in. But it was painful. Luckily, Amsterdam was a good place to recover from such wounds.

In the '80s I got involved in the Goddess movement, which in many ways was really about uncovering hidden histories—or "herstories," as we liked to say back then. In the process I discovered something very important and powerful. Trans people have always existed and more often than not been seen as sacred and powerful. This may seem almost self-evident now, but many people had considered "transsexualism" as a modern phenomenon and usually a negative one—a creation of the medical profession, an offshoot of repressed homosexuality, even a result somehow of what Marxists like to call late capitalism. The discovery of trans people's ancient history became a kind of antidote to all these negative and very limited views.

In the words of Normandi Ellis in her brilliant book *Awakening Osiris* (a poetic translation of the so-called *Egyptian Book of the Dead*), "Give me not words of consolation. Give me magic, the fire of one beyond the borders of enchantment. Give me the spell of living well."

Part of that ancient history included shamanism. I began reading about this long before the term became a cultural phenomenon. Some kind of gender change was so ingrained in tribal shamanism that when people started going to workshops to find their "power animal" and declare themselves shamans,

I always wanted to say to them, "How can you be a shaman if you've never changed sex?"

One of the features of shamanism—and mediums, for that matter—is what the scholar Mircea Eliade called "the shamanic crisis." A young person becomes very ill or suffers what seem to be horrendous hallucinations. The way through this is allow it to happen, to let the demons, or beasts, tear them apart, and then put them back together, but now transformed into a person of power. And as mentioned, the process often involves changing gender.

The experiences became ritualized, and literal, in the more structured world of historical antiquity (and even into contemporary life, with the *hijras* of India and Pakistan). Possibly the most famous ancient example is the *gallae* (unlike many mainstream historians, I use the feminine form of the plural name) who came from Anatolia (Western Turkey) to Rome with their Goddess, Kybele. Standard texts will refer to them as "self-castrated eunuch priests" ("eunuch" is the standard translation of *hijra*). But if they were simply eunuchs, meaning nothing, why did they wear female clothing? In fact, when they healed from their surgery (done in a state of ecstasy), and were initiated into the service of their Goddess, they wore wedding dresses to the ceremony. Kybele's name in Greece was Artemis.

When I was eight or nine I went through a kind of "shamanic crisis" without knowing the concept. Happily, it did not involve flat-out hallucinations, but I experienced terrible nightmares every night. My parents took me to doctors, but no one really knew what to do. (I was lucky—today, the doctors would have fed me drugs.) The nightmares ended when my great-grandmother told my mother to place a small Jewish prayer book under my mattress. My mother did not tell me about it—I did not even know it was there until years later—but the nightmares stopped. This is one reason, but only one, why, whatever else I am—lover of Goddesses, witch, heretic of all sorts—I will always be deeply Jewish.

Out of all those terrible dreams I remembered exactly one. Bears had escaped from the zoo and were rounding up all the humans to imprison us in sewers under the street. I remember being huddled with the other prisoners and looking up through the bars of the sewer grates at the bears gathered around to stare at us. I don't really know why that dream, and only that one, stayed with me for the rest of my life. Or at least I didn't know then.

In the late '80s I went to Greece to research ancient sacred sites for a book called *The Body of the Goddess*. One of the places I went was a temple to Artemis at Brauron, on the southern tip of Attica peninsula. I was interested in Artemis because of the gallae, but also because she was a Goddess of lesbians, and because of a certain mountain formation known in ancient times as "Winged Artemis" (the relationship between landscape and religion was part of the thesis of my book). And also because, in various ways, Artemis had begun to seem a strong presence in my life.

When I got to Brauron, I discovered something fascinating. Preadolescent girls from Athens would be given in service to Artemis, to live a kind of wild life in the temple until they reached the age at which they had to return and get married. While at Brauron they dressed in bear skins rather than "civilized" dresses, and bore the collective title *arctoi*, or "bear cubs." The age when they left the rigid roles of society to become wild bears was nine years old, the same age I was when I had my dream of being "captured" by the bears.

In the '90s I moved back to America and once again became involved with activism. I lectured and wrote articles about trans experience being worldwide and as old as humanity. Ironically, some young activist recently described people who transitioned in the '90s as "prehistoric." I thought, what does that make me, who transitioned in the '70s? Paleolithic? Luckily, Paleolithic cave art is one of my passions.

Along with writing articles, and working with trans groups, I wrote a comic book called *Doom Patrol* (first created in the '60s), in which I introduced a "transsexual lesbian" superhero named Kate Godwin (superhero name "Coagula," though we almost never used it). The name was inspired by two friends of mine, Kate Bornstein and Chelsea Goodwin. Actually the idea for the character came partly from Chelsea. When I told her I was writing a comic book, she said, "Oh, can I be a character? I've always wanted to be a superhero."

I did not see this as a revolutionary act. It just seemed natural to me to include a trans character. These were my friends; why shouldn't they be part of a superhero team? For others, though, it was groundbreaking.

My run on *Doom Patrol* was only two years, but its impact continued, like an underground current, into the lives and works of people not even born when I was writing it. A few years ago I was invited to be a keynote speaker at the world's first "transgender literary conference," held at the University of Winnipeg. I was surprised. I honestly did not think people remembered the work I'd done. When I arrived, I was treated like a pioneer and even a hero, especially by a new generation of cartoonists and comics creators, who saw Kate Godwin as a great inspiration. I spoke for forty minutes, without text or even any notes, and received a standing ovation.

Finally, what does it mean to me to be trans? It means to free yourself, as much as possible, from rigid social structures, other people's judgments, from fear and shame, from history itself. It means to become something that is both completely new and unknowably ancient. It means to discover that the antidote to shame and fear is not assurances that nothing is wrong with you, but passion, for once again, as Nor Hall wrote, "Surrender to the body's desire is itself a form of liberation." It is to discover—or remember—that in the stunning words of cartoonist Chan X. Parker, "Sometimes I feel like I am made of stars. And that nothing short of planets and meteors and nebulas could ever possibly clothe me."

To further quote Normandi Ellis ("Give me not words of consolation. . . . Give me the spell of living well"), "I am the knot where two worlds meet. Red magic courses through me like the blood of Isis, magic of magic, spirit of spirit. I am proof of the power of gods."

Burning Beard
The Dreams and Visions of Joseph ben Jacob, Lord Viceroy of Egypt

"There was a young Hebrew in the prison, a
slave of the captain of the guard. We told him
our dreams and he interpreted them."
—Genesis, 41:12

"Why did you repay good with evil? This is the cup from
which my lord drinks, and which he uses for divination."
—Genesis, 44:5

If   a   Man   Sees   Himself   in   a   Dream

killing an ox: Good. It means the
removal of the dreamer's enemies.
writing on a palette: Good. It means the
establishment of the dreamer's office.
uncovering his backside: Bad. It means the
dreamer will become an orphan.
—Excerpts from Egyptian dream book, found on *recto*,
or back side, of a papyrus from the 19th Dynasty

IN THE LAST MONTH of his life, when his runaway liver has all but eaten his body, Lord Joseph orders his slave to set his flimsy frame upright, like the sacred pillar of the God Osiris in the annual festival of rebirth. Joseph has other things on his mind, however, than his journey to the next world. He has his servant dress him as a Phoenician trader, and then two bearers carry him alone to the dream house behind the temple of Thoth, God of magic, science, writing, celestial navigation, swindlers, gamblers, and dreams. Joseph braces himself against the red column on the outside of the building, then enters with as firm a step as he can. The two interpreters who come to him strike him as hacks, their beards unkempt, their hair dirty, their makeup cracked and sloppy, and their long coats—

It hardly matters that the coats are torn in places, bare in others. Just the sight of those swirls of color floods Joseph's heart with memory. He sees his childhood dream as if he has just woken up from it. The court magicians in their magnificent coats lined up before Pharaoh. The Burning Beard and his brother shouting their demands. The sticks that changed into snakes. And he remembers the coat his mother made for him, the start of all his troubles. And the way he screamed when Judah and Gad tore it off him and drenched it in the blood of some poor ibex they'd caught in one of their traps.

Startled, Joseph realizes the interpreters are speaking to him. "Sir," they say, "how may we serve you?"

"As you see," Joseph says, "I am an old man, on the edge of death. Lately my dreams have troubled me. And where better to seek answers than in Luxor, so renowned for dreamers?" The two smile. Joseph says, "Of course, I would have preferred the interpretations of your famous Joseph"—he watches them wince—"but I am only a merchant, and I am sure Lord Joseph speaks only to princes."

The younger of the two, a man about thirty with slicked down hair says, "Well, he's sick, you know. And there are those who say the Pharaoh's publicity people exaggerate his powers." He adds, with a wave of his hand, "One lucky guess, years ago . . ."

"Tell me," Joseph says, his voice lower, "is he really a Hebrew? I've heard that, but I find it hard to believe."

In a voice even lower, the young one says, "Not only a Hebrew, but a slave. It's true. They plucked him out of prison."

Joseph feigns shock and a slight disgust. "Egypt is certainly more sophisticated than Phoenicia," he says. "In Tyre our slaves sweat for us, not the other way around."

The other stares at the stone cut floor. "Yes," he says. "Well, the Viceroy is old, and things change."

Quickly, the older one says, "Why don't you tell us your dreams?"

"Lately, they've been very—I guess vivid is the best word. Just last night I dreamed I was sailing all alone down a river."

"Ah, good," the older one says. "A sign of wealth to come."

"It had better come soon, or I won't have much use for it. But to continue—I climbed the mast—"

"Wonderful. Your God will bear you aloft with renewed health and good fortune."

Joseph notices their eyes on the purse he carries on his belt. He goes on, "When I came down I became very hungry and ate the first thing I saw, which only afterwards I realized was the offal of animals. I haven't dared to tell anyone of this. Surely this is some omen of destruction."

"Oh no," the younger one jumps in. "In fact, it ensures prosperity."

"Really?" Joseph says. "Then what a lucky dream. Every turn a good omen." He smiles, remembering the fun he had making up the silly dream out of their lists. But the smile fades. He says, "Maybe you can do another one. Actually, this dream has come to me several times in my life." They nod. Joseph knows that the dream books place great emphasis on recurrence. After all, he thinks, if a dream is important enough to come back, maybe the interpreters can charge double.

He closes his eyes for a moment, sighs. When he looks at them again he sees them through a yellow haze of sickness. He begins, "I dream of a man. Very large and frightening. Strangely, his beard appears all on fire."

He can see them race through their catalogues in their minds. Finally the old one says, "Umm, good. It means you will achieve authority in your home."

Joseph says, "But the man is not me."

The young one says, "That doesn't matter."

"I see. Then I'll continue. This man, who dresses as a shepherd but was once a prince, appears before Pharaoh. He demands that Pharaoh surrender to him a vast horde of Pharaoh's subjects." He pauses, but now there is no answer. They look confused. Joseph continues, "When the mob follow the man he promises them paradise but instead leads them into the desert."

"A bad sign?" the old one says tentatively.

Joseph says, "They clamor for food, of course, but instead he leaves them to climb a mountain. And there, in the clouds, he writes a book. He writes it on stone and sheepskin. The history of the world, he calls it. The history and all its laws."

Now there is silence. "Can you help me?" Joseph says. "Should I fear or hope?" The two just stand there. Finally, so tired he can hardly move, Joseph drops the purse on a painted stone table and leaves the temple.

Ten-year-old Joseph wants to open a school for diviners. "Prophecy, dreams interpreted, plan for the future," his announcements will say. And under a portrait of him, "Lord Joseph, Reader and Advisor." Reuben, his oldest brother, shakes his head in disgust. Small flecks of mud fly out of his beard and into Poppa Jacob's lentils. Reuben says, "What does that mean, reader and advisor? Since when do you know how to read?"

Joseph blushes. "I'm going to learn," he says. Over Reuben's laugh he adds quickly, "Anyway, when I see the future, that's a kind of reading. The dreams and the pictures I see in the wine. That's just like reading."

Reuben snorts his disgust. To their father he says, "If you'd make him do some decent work, he wouldn't act this way."

Rachel is about to say something, but Joseph looks at her with his please-mother-I-can-handle-this-myself look. He says, "Divining is work. Didn't that Phoenician woman give me a basket of pomegranates for finding her cat?"

Under his breath, Reuben mutters, "Rotten pomegranates. And why would anyone want a cat, for Yah's sake?"

But Joseph ignores him. He can see he's got the old man's attention. "And we can sell things," he adds. "Open a shop."

"A shop?" Jacob says. His nostrils flare slightly in alarm.

"Sure," Joseph says, not noticing his mother's signal to stop. "When people study with me they'll need equipment. Colored coats, cups to pour the wine, even books. I can write instruction books. 'The Interpretation of Dreams.' That's when I learn to read, of course."

Jacob spits on the rug, an act that makes Rachel turn her face. "We are not merchants," he says. "Damnit, maybe your brothers are right." He ignores his wife's stagy whisper, "Half brothers," and goes on, "Maybe you need to get your fingers in some sheep, slap some mud on that pretty face of yours."

Before Joseph can make it worse Rachel covers his mouth and pulls him outside.

Over the laughter of the brothers, Judah yells, "Goodbye, Lord Joseph. See you in the sheep dung!"

Rachel makes sure Joseph wraps his coat around him against the desert's bite. Even under the thin light of the stars, the waves of color flicker as if alive. What wonderful dreams this boy has, she thinks. She remembers the morning he demanded the coat. Needed it for his work, he said. Leah's brats tried to stop it being made, of course, but Rachel won. Just like always. She says, "Those loudmouths. How dare they laugh at you? You are a lord. A true prince compared to them."

But Joseph pays her no attention. Instead, he stares at the planets, Venus and Jupiter, as bright as fire, hanging from the skin of a half-dead Moon. Images fall from them, as if from holes in the storage house of night.

He sees a lion, a great beast, except it changes, becomes a cub, its fur a wave of light. Seraphs come down, those fake men with the leathery wings that Joseph's father saw in his dream climbing up and down that ladder to heaven and never thought to shout at them, "Why don't you just fly?" The seraphs place a crown like a baby sun on the lion's head. And then they just fly away, as if they have done their job. No, Joseph wants to scream at them, don't leave me. For already he can see them. The wild dogs. They climb up from holes in the Earth, they cover the lion, tear holes in his skin, spit into his eyes.

Joseph slams his own eyes with the heels of his hands. The trick works, for suddenly he becomes aware of his mother beside him, her worry a bright mark on her face as she wipes a drop of spit from his open mouth. Vaguely, he pushes her hand away. Now the tail comes, he thinks. The bit of clean information after the torrent of pictures. Just as his brothers begin to leave their father's grand tent, it hits Joseph, so hard he staggers backward. They want to kill him. If they could, they would tie him to a rock and slit him open, the way his great-grandfather Abraham tried to kill Grandpa Isaac, and even struggled against the—seraph?—that held his hand and shouted in his ear to stop, stop, it was over, Yah had changed His mind. Yet in all the terror, Joseph can't help but smirk, for he realizes something further. Reuben, Reuben, will stop them.

"What are you laughing at?" Reuben says as he marches past, and it's all Joseph can do not to really laugh, for it almost doesn't matter, scary as it is. He knows something about them that they don't even know themselves. And doesn't that make him their lord?

Mostly Joseph divines from dreams, but sometimes the cup shows him what he needs to know. His mother gave him the cup when he was five. She'd ordered it made two years before, when their travels took them past the old woman who kept the kiln outside Luz. Rachel had had her own dream of how it should look, with rainbow swirls in the glaze, and four knobs of different colors. It took a long time but she made Jacob wait, despite the older boys' complaints, until the potter finished it. And then Rachel put it aside until the ceremony by the fire, when Joseph's first haircut would turn him from a wild animal (one who secretly still sucked at his mother) into a human. Rachel couldn't attend—yet another boys' only event—but they came and told her what happened—how he whooped it up, jumping and waving his arms like a cross between a monkey and a bat, how his hair made the fire flare so that Jacob had to yank the child back to keep him from getting scorched. And then how Joseph quieted when his father gave him the cup, how he purred over it like a girl, how his father poured the wine. But instead of drinking Joseph just stared at it, stared and made a noise like a nightmare, and might have flung it away if Jacob hadn't grabbed hold of him (a salvation Jacob later regretted) and forced him to drink the wine so they could end the ceremony.

It took Rachel a long time to get Joseph to tell her what he'd seen. Darkness, he said finally. Darkness over all the world, thicker than smoke. And a hand in the dark sky, a finger outstretched, reaching, reaching, stroking invisible foreheads. He heard cries, he said, shrieks and wails in the blackness. Then light came—and everywhere, in every home, from palace to shack, women held their dead children against their bodies. "I'm not going to die, am I?" Joseph asked her.

"No, no, darling, it's not for you, it's for someone else. The bad people. Don't worry, sweetie, it's not for you." Joseph cried and cried while his mother held him and kissed the torn remnants of his hair.

As much as they make fun of him, as much as they complain to Jacob about his airs and his lack of work, the brothers will sometimes sneak into his tent, after they think everyone has fallen asleep. "Can you find my staff?" they'll say, or "Who's this Ugarit girl Pop's got lined up for me? Is she good-looking? Can she keep her mouth shut?" The wives come even more often, scurrying along the path as if anyone who saw them would mistake them for rabbits. "Tell me it's going to be a boy," they say, "Please, he'll kill me if it's another girl," as if the diviner can control something like that, as if events are at the mercy of the diviner, and not the other way around.

At first, Joseph soaks in their secret devotions. When Zebulon ridicules him, Joseph looks him in the eye, as if to say, "Put on a good show, big brother, because you know and I know what you think about after dark, under your sheepskin." Or maybe he'll just finger the colored stone Zeb gave him as a bribe not to say anything. But after a while he wishes they'd leave him alone. He even pretends to sleep, but they just grab him by the shoulder. Worst of all are the ones who offer themselves to him, not just the wives, but sometimes the brothers too, pretending it's something Joseph is longing for. Do they do it just to reward him, or because they really desire him, or because they think of it as some kind of magic that will change a bad prediction? Joseph tries to find the answer in his cup, or a dream, but the wine and the night remain as blank as his brothers' faces. He can see the fate of entire tribes but not the motives of his own brothers. Maybe there are no motives. Maybe people do things for no reason at all.

And Joseph himself? Why does he do it? Just to know things other people don't? To make himself better than his brothers? Because he can? Because he can't stop himself? As a child he loves the excitement, that lick of fire that sometimes becomes a whip. Later, especially the last days in Egypt, he wishes it would end. His body can't take the shock, his mind can't take the knowledge. He prays, he sacrifices goats stolen from the palace herd and smuggled into the desert. No use. The visions keep coming, wanted or not.

Only near the very end of his life does he get an answer. The half burnt goat sends up a shimmer of light that Joseph stares at, hypnotized, so that he doesn't hear the desert roar, or see the swirl of sand that marks a storm until it literally slaps him in the face. He cowers down and covers himself as best he can, and wonders if he will die here so that no one will ever find his body. Maybe his family will think Yah just sucked him up into heaven, too impatient to wait for Joseph to die. In the midst of it all, he hears it. The Voice. An actual voice! High pitched, somewhere between a man and a woman, it shouts at him out of the whirlwind. "Do you think I do this for *you*? I opened secrets for you because I *needed* you. I will close them when I close them!"

The fact is, Joseph is no fool. By his final years, he's known for a long time that Yah has used him. He doesn't like that this bothers him, but it does. A messenger, he tells himself. A filler. A bridge between his father and the other one, the Burning Beard. He knows exactly what people will think over the millennia. Jacob will get ranked as the last patriarch (the only real patriarch, Joseph thinks, the only one to pump out enough boys to found a nation), the other one the Great Leader. And Joseph? A clever bureaucrat. A nice guy who lured his family to Egypt and left them there to get into trouble.

He considers writing his own story. "The Life of Joseph ben Jacob, Lord Viceroy of Egypt." But what good would it do? A fire would incinerate the papyrus, or a desert lion would claw it to shreds, or maybe a freak flood would wash away the hieroglyphs. By whatever means, Yah would make sure no one would ever see it. The Beard is the writer, after all. God's scribe.

Some things Joseph knows from the ripples and colors of the wine. Others require a dream. He first sees the man he calls "the Beard" in a dream. Joseph is eight, a spindly brat with a squeaky voice. He's had a bad evening, swatted by Simeon for a trick he'd played on Levi. In despair that no one loves him, he drinks down a whole cup of wine from the flask his mother has given him. The cup falls with a thud on the dirt floor of his tent as he instantly falls down asleep.

At first, he sees only the flame. It fills his dream like floodwaters hitting a dry riverbed. Finally, Joseph and the fire separate so that he can see it as a blaze on a man's face. No, not the face, the beard. The man has thick eyebrows and thin hair, and sad eyes, and a beard bushier than Reuben's, except the beard is on fire! The flames roar all about the face and neck, yet somehow never seem to hurt him. They don't even seem to consume anything; his beard always stays the same. Later in life, in countless dreams, Joseph will study this man and the inferno on his face. He will wonder if maybe the fire is an illusion—the man's a master magician, after all—or a trick of the desert light (except it looks the same inside Pharaoh's palace). And he will wonder why no one ever seems to notice it, not the Pharaoh, not the Beard's self-serving brother, not the whiny mob that follows him through the desert. In that first time, however, the fiery beard scares him so much he can only hide in the corner of his dream, hardly even aware that the man stands on a dark mountain scorched by lightning, and talks to the clouds.

Joseph doesn't like this man. He doesn't like his haughty pretension of modesty, the I'm-just-a-poor-shepherd routine. He detests the man's willingness to slaughter hordes of his own people just for the sake of discipline. He dislikes his speeches that go on for hours and hours, in that thick slurry voice, always with the same message, obey, obey, obey. Joseph distrusts the man's total lack of humor, his equal lack of respect for women. Can't he see that his sister controls the waters, so that without her to make the rocks sweat they would all die of thirst? As far as Joseph can tell, the mob would have done a lot better if they had followed the sister and not the Beard. Joseph thinks of her as his proper heir as leader of the Hebrews. But then, he has to admit, he always did like women better.

Most of all, Joseph detests the Beard's penchant for self-punishment. The way he lies down in the dirt, cutting his face on the pebbles, the way he'll swear off sex but won't give his wife permission to take anyone else. And what about his hunger strikes that go on for days and days, as if Yah can't stand the smell of food on a man's breath? It might not bother Joseph so much if the man wasn't such a role model for his people. *Joseph's* people. Doesn't the man know that Joseph saved his family—the mob's ancestors, after all—and all of Egypt from starvation just a few generations before? It was Joseph who explained Pharaoh's dream of the seven fat cows and the seven lean ones, Joseph who took over Egypt's food storage systems during the seven good years, building up the stocks for the seven years of famine. It was Joseph who took in his family and fed them so the tribes could survive. Doesn't the Beard know all this? He claims to know everything, doesn't he? The man who talks to Yah. How dare he denounce food? How *dare* he?

Some dreams come so quickly they seem to pounce on him the moment he closes his eyes. Others lie in wait all night until they seize him just before he plans to wake up. The dream of the coat comes that way. Joseph has fidgeted in his sleep for hours, flinging out his arm as if trying to push something away. And then at dawn, just as Reuben and Judah and Issachar and Zebulon are gulping down stony bread on their way to the sheep, their little brother dreams once more of the Burning Beard. He sees the Beard stride into the biggest room Joseph has ever seen. Stone columns thicker than Jacob's ancient ram hold up a roof higher than the Moon. The Beard comes with his brother, who has slicked down his hair and oiled his beard, and wears a silver plate around his neck, obviously more aware than the Beard of how you dress when you appear before a king. Or maybe the Beard has deliberately crafted his appearance, his torn muddy robe, his matted hair, as either contempt for the Pharaoh or a declaration of his own humility. "Look at me, I'm just a country bumpkin, a simple shepherd on an errand for God." Later, in other dreams, Joseph will learn just how staged this act is from the man who grew up as Pharaoh's adopted son. Now, however, the dreaming boy knows only the gleam of the throne room and the scowl of the invader.

The brothers speak together. Though Joseph cannot follow any of it (he will not learn Egyptian for another twenty years) he understands that the Beard has something wrong with his speech so that silver-plate needs to interpret for him. Whatever they say, it certainly bothers the king, who shouts at them and holds up some gold bauble like a protection against the evil eye. The Beard says something to his brother, who strangely throws his shepherd's staff on the floor. Have they surrendered? But no, it's a trick, and a pretty good one, because the stick surrenders its rigidity and becomes a snake!

Asleep, Joseph still shivers under his sheepskin. The king, however, shouts something at one of his toadies who then rushes away, to return a moment later with a whole squad of magicians in the most amazing coats Joseph has ever seen. For Joseph the rest of the dream slides by in a blur—the king's magicians turn their sticks into snakes too only to have silver-plate's snake gobble them up like a basket of honeycakes—because he cannot take his dream eyes off those coats. Panels of linen overlaid with braids of wool, every piece a different color, and hung with charms and talismans of stone and metal. I want that, the dream Joseph thinks to himself, and "I've got to have that," he says out loud the moment he wakes up.

He begins his campaign that very day, whining and posturing and even refusing to eat (later, he will blame the

Beard for this fasting, as if his dreams infected him) until he wins over first his mother and then at last his father. With Jacob on his side, Joseph can ignore the complaints of his brothers, who claim it makes Joseph look like "a Hittite whore."

Joseph doesn't try for the talismans. Jacob probably could afford it, but Joseph knows his limits. Besides, it's the coat he cares about, all the colors, even more swirls than his cup of dreams. The day he gets it he struts all about the camp, the sides of it held open like the fan of a peacock—or maybe like a foolish baboon who does not know enough to protect his chest from his enemies.

That same night, Joseph dreams of the coat soaked in blood.

Joseph's dream power comes from his mother. "All power comes from mothers," Rachel tells him, and thereby sets aside the story Jacob likes, that Yah taught dream interpretation to Adam, who taught it to Seth, who taught it to Noah, whose animals dreamed every night on the boat, only to lose the knack when they walked down the ramp back onto the sodden earth. "Listen to me," Rachel whispers, "you think great men like Adam spent their time with dreams? It was Eve. And she didn't learn it from God, she learned it from the serpent. She bit into the apple and snipped off the head of a worm. And that's when people started to dream."

Joseph's worst moment comes in prison. He sits on his tailbone with his legs drawn up and his arms around his knees, trying to let as little of his body as possible touch the mud and slime of the floor. He's tried so hard, it's so unfair. No matter what terrible tricks Yah played on him—his brothers' hatred, his coat taken from him and streaked with blood—he's done his best, he's accepted it, really he has. And now this! And all because he tried to do something right. When your master's wife wants to screw you, you're supposed to say no, right? Isn't that what Yah teaches (not that it's ever stopped Jacob, but that's not the point)? And instead of a reward he has to sit in garbage and eat worse.

Something touches Joseph's sleeve. He screams and jerks back, certain it's a rat. But when he opens his eyes he sees two men not much older than himself. They wear linen and their hair is curled, signs they've fallen from a high place. "Please," one says, "You're the Hebrew who interprets dreams, aren't you? Will you help us? Please?"

"No," Joseph says. "Go away, leave me alone." Yet he feels a certain tug of pleasure that his reputation as Potiphar's dream speaker has followed him into hell. He tries to ignore them, but they just stand there, looking so desperate, that finally he says, "Oh all right. Tell me your dreams."

The one who goes first announces that he was Pharaoh's chief wine steward before the court gossips slid him into jail. He tells Joseph, "In my dream I saw—I was in a garden. It was nighttime, I think. I looked up high and saw three branches. They began to bud. Blossoms shot forth. There were three ripe grapes. Suddenly, Pharaoh's cup was in my hand. Or maybe it was there before, I'm not sure. I squeezed the grapes in my hand. I poured the juice into the cup. I gave it to Pharaoh. He was just there and I gave it to him and he drank it."

Joseph rolls his eyes. This is not exactly a great mystery, he thinks. He says, "All right, here's the meaning. In three days Pharaoh will lift up your head. He will examine your case and restore you to your office. You'll be safe from this filth and back in the palace. Congratulations."

The man claps his hands. "Blessed Mother Isis!" he cries. "Thank you!" He bends down to kiss Joseph's knees but Joseph pulls his legs even closer to his chest.

"Just promise me something," Joseph says. "When you're back pouring wine for Pharaoh, remember me? Tell him I don't deserve this."

"Oh yes," the man says, and claps his hands again.

"Now me," the other one says. He kneels down before Joseph and says, "In my dream I'm walking in the street behind the palace. There are three baskets on top of my head. Two of them are filled with white bread, but the one on top holds all the lovely things I bake for Pharaoh. Cakes shaped like Horus, a spelt bun like the belly of Hathor. Just as I'm thinking about how much the king will like them, birds come and pluck them away." He laughs, as if he's told a joke. "Right out of the basket. Now," he says, "tell me the meaning."

Joseph stares at him. He stares and stares at the man's eager face. Why has Yah done this to me, he thinks, but even that last shred of self-pity drains out of him, washed away in horror at such pathetic innocence.

"Go on, go on," the man insists.

Can he fake it? Joseph wonders. He tries to think of some story but his mind jams. He can't escape. Yah has set the truth on him like a pack of dogs. In a cracked whisper he says, "In three days Pharaoh shall lift your head from your shoulders. He will hang you from a tree and the birds will eat your body."

The baker doesn't scream, only makes a noise deep in his chest. "Oh Gods," he says, "help me. Help me, please."

Joseph is stunned. No anger, no hate. No demands to change it or make it go away or even to think again. Just that trust. Without thought, Joseph wraps his arms around the man like a mother. "I'm sorry," he says, "I'm so sorry."

Joseph will stay two years in the prison before Pharaoh will dream a dream not found anywhere in the catalogues, and his wine steward, hearing of lean cows and fat cows, will remember the man he had promised not to forget. In all those months, Joseph will think of that empty promise only three or four times. But he will see the face of the baker every morning, before he opens his eyes.

People at court sometimes joke about the Viceroy's clay cup. Childish, they call it. Primitive. Hebrew. Visitors from Kush or Mesopotamia look shocked when they see him raise it in honor of Pharaoh's health. Their advance men, whose job it is to know all the gossip, whisper to them that Lord Joseph uses this cup to divine the future. Perhaps he sees visions in the wine, they say. Or perhaps—these are the views of the more scientifically minded—some impurity in the clay flakes off into the liquid and induces heightened states of awareness. The visitors shake their heads. That's all well and good, they say. He saved Egypt from famine, after all. But why does he drink from it in public?

During long dinners the Viceroy, like other men, will sometimes pause to swirl his barley wine, or else just stare blankly into his cup. At such times, all conversation, all breathing, stops, until Lord Joseph once more lifts up his eyes and makes some bland comment.

The princes, the courtiers, and the slaves all agree. The God Thoth visits Joseph at night, when together they discuss the secrets of the universe. A bright light leaks under the door of the Viceroy's bedchamber, and sometimes an alert slave will hear the flutter of Thoth's wings. And sometimes, they say, Thoth himself becomes the student, silent with wonder as Joseph teaches him secrets beyond the knowledge of Gods.

———

The boy Joseph curls himself up in the pit where his brothers have thrown him. Frozen in the desert night without his coat, he clutches the one treasure they didn't take from him, the cup his mother gave him, which he keeps always in a pouch on a cord around his waist. What will it be? A lion, a scorpion, a snake? Instead, before Judah and Simeon come back to sell him as a slave, a deep sleep takes him. He does not know it, but Yah has covered him with a foul smell that will drive away the beasts, for now is the time to dream. Joseph sees himself standing before a dark sky, with his arms out and his face lifted. A crown appears on his head. The crown becomes light, pure light that spreads through his body—his forehead, his mouth, his shoulders, all the way to his fingertips, light that streams out of him, through his heart and his lungs, even his entrails, if he shits he shits light, his penis ejaculates light, the muscles and bones of his legs pure light, his toes on fire with light. Joseph tries to cry out, but light rivers from his mouth.

And then it shatters. Broken light, broken Joseph splashes through the world, becomes darkness, becomes dust, becomes bodies and rock, light encased in darkness and bodies. And letters. Letters that fall from the sky, like drops of black flame.

Joseph wakes to the hands of the slave traders dragging him up from the dirt.

Does the Beard dream? Does the fire on his face allow him even to sleep? Or does he spend so much time chatting with

Yah, punishing slackers, and writing, writing, writing, that he looks at dreams, and even the future, as a hobby for children and weak minds? After all, what does the Beard care about the future? He has his book. For him, time ends with the final letter.

When his brothers bully him, when they throw mud on his coat or trip him so he falls on pebbles sharp enough to splash his coat with blood, Joseph just wants to get back at them. In Jacob's tent one night he decides to make up a prophecy. "Listen, everybody," he announces. "I had a dream. Last night. A really good one." They roll their eyes or make faces but no one stops him. They don't want to believe in him, but they do. "Here it is," he says gleefully. "All of us were out in the fields binding sheaves. We stepped back from them, but my sheaf stood upright and all yours bowed down to it." He smiles. "What do you think?"

Silence. No one wants to look at anyone. At last, Reuben says, "Since when do you ever go out and bind sheaves?" Inside their laughter, Joseph hears the whisper of fear.

That night, a dream comes to him. The Sun, the Moon, and eleven stars all bow down to him. He wakes up more scared than elated. He should keep it to himself, he knows. He's already got them mad, who knows what they'll do if he pushes this one at them. He pours some water into his cup from the gourd his mother's handmaids fill for him. Before he can drink, however, he sees in the bubbles everything that will follow—how the dream will provoke his brothers, how he will become a slave in Egypt, how he will rise to viceroy so that his family and in fact all Egypt will bow to him. It will not last, he sees. Their descendants will all become slaves, only to get free once more and stumble through the desert for forty years, *forty years*, before they can get back to their homeland. The vision doesn't last. Startled, he spills the water, and the details spill from his brain. Yet he knows now that everything leads to something else, that all his actions serve some secret purpose known only to Yah. Is it all just tricks, then? Do Yah's schemes ever come to an end?

He can stop it, he knows. All he has to do is never tell anyone the dream. Doesn't Grandpa Isaac claim God gives all of us free will? (He remembers his father whispering, "All except my brother Esau. He's too stupid.") If Joseph just keeps silent, the whole routine can never get started.

That afternoon, Zebulon kicks him and he blurts out, "You think you're so strong? I dreamed that the Sun and Moon and eleven stars all bowed down to me. That's right, eleven. What do you think of that?"

Joseph is old now, facing the blank door of death. He has blessed his children and his grandchildren and their children. Soon, he knows, the embalmers will suck out his brains, squirt the "blood of Thoth" into his body, wrap him in bandages, and encase him in stone. He wonders—if his descendants really do leave Egypt, will they find him and drag him along with them?

At the foot of his bed lies a wool and linen coat painted in swirls of color. Joseph has no idea how it got there. By the size of it, it looks made for a boy, or maybe a shrunken old man. Next to the bed, on a little stand, sits his cup, as bright as the coat. He has told his slave to fill it with wine, though Joseph knows he lacks the strength to lift it, let alone pour it down his throat.

When he dies, will he see Rachel and Jacob? Or has he waited so long they've grown impatient and wandered off somewhere he will never find them? He is alone now. The doctors and the magicians, his family, his servants, he's ordered them all away, and to his surprise they have listened. He wants more than anything to stay awake, so he can feel his soul, his ka, as the Egyptians call it, rattle around inside his body until it finds the way out. He tells himself that he's read all the papyruses, the "books of the dead," and wants to find out for himself. But he knows the real reason to stay awake. He doesn't want any more dreams. As always, however, Yah makes His own plans.

In his dream, Joseph sees the Burning Beard one more time. With his face even more of a blaze than usual, he and his brother accost Pharaoh in the early morning, when Pharaoh goes down to wash in the Nile. Joseph watches them argue, but all he can hear is a roar. Now the brother raises his staff, he strikes the water—and the Nile turns to blood! Joseph shouts but does not wake up. All over Egypt, he sees, water has turned to blood, not just the river but the streams and the reservoirs and even the wells. For days it goes on, with the old, the young, and the weak dying of thirst. Finally the water returns.

Only—frogs return with it. The entire Nile swarms with them. Soon they cover people's tables, their food, their bodies. And still more horrors follow. The brother strikes the dust and lice spring forth. Wild beasts roar in from the desert.

Joseph twists in agony, but Yah will not release him. He sees both brothers take fistfuls of furnace ash and throw them into the sky. A wind blows the ash over all the people of Egypt, and where it touches the skin, boils erupt. Now the Beard lifts his arms to the sky and hail kills every creature unfortunate enough to be standing outside. As if he has not done enough he spreads his hands at night and calls up an east wind to bring swarms of locusts. They eat whatever crops the hail has left standing. No, Joseph cries. I saved these people from famine. Don't do this. He can only watch as the Beard lifts his hand and pulls down three days of darkness.

And then—and then—when the darkness lifts, the first born of every woman and animal, from Pharaoh's wives and handmaids to the simplest farm slave who could never affect political decisions in any way, even the cows and the sheep and the chickens, the first born of every one of them falls down dead.

Just at the moment of waking up, Joseph sees that the finger of death has spared certain houses, those marked with a smear of lamb's blood. The Hebrews. Yah and the Beard have saved the Hebrews. Joseph's people. But aren't the Egyptians Joseph's people as well? And didn't he bring the Hebrews to Egypt? If all this carnage comes because the Hebrews have lived in Egypt, is it all Joseph's fault?

He wakes up choking. For the first time in days his eyes find the strength to weep. He wishes he could get up and kneel by the bed, but since he cannot he prays on his back. "Please," he whispers. "I have never asked You for anything. Not really. Now I am begging You. Make me wrong. Make this one dream false. Make all my powers a lie. Take my gift and wipe it from the world. Do anything, anything, but please, please, make me wrong."

But he knows it will not happen. He is Joseph ben Jacob, Lord Viceroy of dreams. And he has never made a wrong prediction in his life.

"Radical, Sacred, Hopefully Magical"
Rachel Pollack interviewed by Terry Bisson

Does Tarot work?

Yes. Not only that, it will do the work you hire it to do. It has a long resumé.

Your career with Tarot seems quite successful. Do your followers know you are also a fiction writer? Is there leakage between the two realms?

Not that much, which I find both strange and frustrating. Strange, because you'd think that people who say that my Tarot books are vital to their lives would be very interested to read my stories (since Tarot is somewhat specialized, I would not necessarily expect that of my fiction audience). But that does not seem to be the case. And frustrating, both because who doesn't want a wider audience, and I think people's views on Tarot might open up somewhat to read my fiction. I am the same person, after all. I don't turn a switch in my brain to write one, then the other.

The Shining Tribe artwork—yours? Are the cards different? How much alteration and invention is acceptable?

Yes. I had planned to sketch them out, then hire an artist to do the final pictures. But I had trouble finding someone who was willing to stay close to my visions of what they should be. Then the great artist Niki de Saint Phalle, who had invited me to consult with her on her Tarot sculpture garden in Italy, told me I needed to do them myself. So I became more serious about the drawing. The influences are to a large extent tribal and prehistoric art from around the world, but they're also connected thematically to the more well-known versions of the cards. Not everyone sees that, however, which has caused some people to think they cannot "work" with the deck. Something I find very satisfying is that the strongest response to the pictures has come from artists.

What's a Traveler? What do you think of the movie The Fisher King?

The Travelers are meant to be the reality behind all the traditions of sorcerers, magicians, witches, shamans, root doctors, alchemists, etc., from the earliest humans to the present day. They are always set apart, keeping their existence hidden from ordinary society, yet also completely up to date, having their own dark web, called Jinn-net, and using "spirit drones" to deliver supplies for their magical workings. I've had a great time writing these stories. Each one adds to the lore, building on the ones before it.

I love *The Fisher King*—seen it three times. Mostly it's the brilliant construction and the powerful performances, but I also found it thrilling because I studied King Arthur in college and know the original story of the Fisher King and the Wasteland. The title of my Jack Shade collection, *The Fissure King*, actually came from a writer friend named Nancy Norbeck. We were discussing a *Doctor Who* episode with an alien called the Fisher King, and Nancy said that the first time she heard a character say it she took it as "Fissure." I realized that the expression, as both a title and a character, was perfect for an original novella that would tie together the four previously published stories. I asked if I could use it, and Nancy was kind enough to agree.

What or who got you into Tarot? Or were you raised in that religion?

As I'm sure you know, Tarot is not a religion. It began as a card game in the Renaissance, then in the late eighteenth century it began to be seen as both a repository for ancient doctrines and a device for fortune-telling. Growing up, I never heard of it, and even after college I only knew of it as a sort of plot device in T.S. Eliot's great poem "The Wasteland" (which is based on the Fisher King, among other things). Then, in the early spring of 1970, I was teaching at a state college in upstate New York, and another teacher said she would read my Tarot cards if I gave her a ride home. As soon as I saw them I knew they were something I had to have. They were pretty obscure back then, and it took some searching but I finally found a deck.

That time, 1970–71, was a great watershed for me. I discovered the Tarot (or the Tarot discovered me), I came out as a transwoman and a lesbian, and I sold my first story, to Michael Moorcock's *New Worlds*.

What are the two parts of Why?
Origins and purpose.

Why does the Sun exist? Because pieces of dead stars coalesced to form a next-generation star that reached a critical mass and came to life.

Why does the Sun exist? To create just the right conditions for organic, self-aware life to come into existence on the third planet, and with life, eventually, consciousness.

Who was Lou Stathis?
My second editor on the comic *Doom Patrol*. Lou was tough. I learned a lot from him, but he also was a champion of my work. Sadly, he died, way too young, of a rare brain condition inherited from his father (who'd also died of it), and the editor who took over had a different vision of what kind of work he wanted to see.

You have been acclaimed as "One of the Most Important Women in Geek History." Gosh. Does this come with benefits?

Ah, if only. The fact is, though, there is a great benefit, and that is hearing from the people whose lives my work has touched. I also get invited to teach (usually Tarot) in places like Australia and China, and that's pretty terrific.

Tell us about Doom Patrol. *How did that come about?*
I greatly admired the work being done on it in the late '80s (the comic began in the '60s), by a writer-artist team named Grant Morrison and Richard Case. At a party I met the editor, Tom Peyer, and after gushing about it confessed it was (then) the only monthly comic I really wished I might someday have a chance to write. Tom told me that Grant was ending his run, and if I wanted to send him a sample script he'd consider it. So I did, and it became my first issue. In the months leading up to the change-over I wrote a series of dumb letters in the voice of a gee-whiz fangirl. The first said something like "Gee, Mr. Peyer, *Doom Patrol* is just the coolest thing ever!!! Grant Morrison is, like, totally a complete genius!!! If he gets sick or dies or something, can I write it?" I sent the first to Tom without telling him, and he liked it so much he told me to send one every month until the time came to make the announcement. In the next to last one I threatened him with some kind of mob action (his head in the toilet bowl, I think I said) unless he let me write it. Then in the last I apologized, adding, "The thing is, I already told my mom I was doing it, and she told all her friends." So Tom, as the editor, announced, "Well, there it is,

she told her mom, so what can we do? Rachel Pollack is the new writer on *Doom Patrol*." And amazingly, there are people to this day who believe that's how I got the job.

A historian of comix (there are many) once said that your character Coagula "perfectly explained to Robotman how gender identity works." What did she tell him?

First of all, a nitpick—"comix" refers to the "underground" work by 1960s–70s cartoonists, such as R. Crumb. The work published by the big companies has always been called "comics." Coagula, whose actual name was Kate Godwin (we almost never used the secret hero name—the characters in *Doom Patrol* didn't have secret identities) doesn't so much explain gender identity to Cliff (Robotman) as identity itself. Though Cliff is a human brain in a metal robot body, he's been falling for Kate, and then someone tells him she's trans. He freaks out and confronts her, saying, "You used to be a man!" Kate says, "No, Cliff, I was never a man." Then he says, "But you had a penis, right? And you cut it off!" Kate then says, "And what about you, Cliff? Do you have a penis? Are you a man?" She then goes on to say we are who we are because we know who we are.

What were her superpowers?

She had alchemical powers based on the old slogan "Solve et Coagula." A gesture with her left hand could make something dissolve, then the right could cause it to coagulate. But really, her main superpower was belief in herself.

If, as some believe, science fiction is a bastard child of literature, then comics are . . .
The bastard child of movies? Or maybe it's the other way around. Not sure.

What kind of car do you drive? I ask this of everyone.
A red Nissan Versa named Katrina (for the mysterious "High T" in the title story of this collection).

Did you enter the SF/Fantasy field as a fan or as a writer? Were you made to feel welcome?
Oddly enough, I did not know fandom existed until I became a pro writer. I wish I had, I'm sure my high school and college years would have been a lot more exciting. And I was definitely welcomed.

Is there a lot of paperwork involved in gender change? Licenses, deeds, IDs, etc.?
Not as much now as there used to be! Or maybe it's just a lot easier.

What poets do you read for fun?

Questions like this always throw me because it changes—and because I read more prose. I've liked Joy Harjo a lot—Muscogee (Creek) poet who writes in English. And I was, am, very influenced by a movement called Ethnopoetics, radical modern translations of ancient poetry and shamanic/magical texts. There's an experimental poet/fiction writer named Selah Saterstrom I enjoy. Her work is influenced by magic and divination. I read "The Wasteland" every April ("the cruelest month") and short passages from *Finnegans Wake* every February 2, which is James Joyce's birthday. Technically, the *Wake* is a novel, but its language is more musical than any poetry.

What pulled you into writing, story or words?
Tough one. I would have to say story, but the way it's told is so vital.

Is "Burning Beard" from the Bible, or does it only pretend to be?
Well, it's what Jews call *midrash*, a kind of expansion of something in the Bible, in this case the life story of Joseph, from Genesis. But it's a pretty radical form of midrash!

I think of you as a "stand-aside" writer. I expect a certain formality in your prose, which elevates everything. Even the humor.
I like that. Thanks. The only thing I'd add is that I think I do that even more with strong emotions, particularly in parts of "The Beatrix Gates."

Ever hit a bad patch in either career?

When *Godmother Night* won the World Fantasy Award it was already out of print, and its American editor, who was a champion of my work, told me that the publisher had told him there was "no way" they'd publish another fantasy by me.

You write in longhand first with a fountain pen. Any other drills, charms, or tricks as a writer?

Just pushing myself to write a certain number of words a day. I sometimes like to say, "Anyone who thinks guilt never helps anything has never been a writer."

What were you doing in 1968?

Marching, shouting, chanting. Actually, I was in grad school for a year, which was awful. I also cast my first presidential vote. I couldn't bring myself to vote for Hubert Humphrey, so voted for the radical black comic Dick Gregory. Later I found out that Gregory, for all his terrific politics on many issues, was an anti-Semite. That was a lesson I never forgot.

Your first publication was with a pen name. How come and what was it?

Not really a pen name, just my birth name. I sold my first story before I came out and changed my name. And as I say in the essay "Trans Central Station," you can find it easily enough, but I'm not going to give it, out of respect for all those trans people who must fight so hard for people to acknowledge their "real" name, the name they give themselves.

Shamanism, Tarot, Judaism, Paganism, Witchery—are all these present in your everyday quotidian life or are you just saving a seat for them?
You forgot Goddess worship! They're all there, but in my own mix. A friend once told me of a form that asked your "faith," and I thought, if I had to answer that, I might put down "Heresy."

You had an encounter with cancer. Anything to say about that? Turning point, hinge, bump in the road?
It was an amazing experience, largely due to the great out-pouring of love and support from so many people literally all over the world. I had cancer twice, actually, with the second time requiring a very radical treatment known as "stem cell replacement therapy," requiring three weeks in the hospital. But it's two years now, and it seems to have worked.

I know you have a suspicion that certain science fiction writers were secretly trans. Care to comment? Why not?
I like that "Why not?" It's respect, really, for people's privacy, in this case mostly the families, since two of them are dead.

And I get this from their writings, not any knowledge of their private lives.

My Jeopardy *answer: Young Adult. You provide the question.*
"What is the most dismissed subgenre in writing today?" The finest book about slavery ever written by a white person is a YA book, *The Astonishing Life of Octavian Nothing, Traitor to the Nation*, by M.T. Anderson. And one of the greatest fantasy works of modern literature, *His Dark Materials* by Philip Pullman, is not even YA, it's a children's book.

Violets were once big business in Rhinebeck. Also, Rufus Wainwright was born there. Is there a connection?
Didn't know about the violets, but Rufus Wainwright's mother, Kate McGarrigle, wrote one of my favorite songs, "Talk to Me of Mendocino."

One sentence on each please: Guy Davenport, Marion Zimmer Bradley, Ray Lafferty.
Pass on the first two. For the third, R.A. Lafferty is one of the great neglected writers of SF, somewhat like Cordwainer Smith. My partner and I used to refer to him as Great-Souled Lafferty. (That's two sentences, but I figure I had credit from the other two writers.)

Ever been torn apart by wild dogs?

Keep thinking I should say yes, but nothing comes to mind.

Rejected by (or disappointed in?) mainstream feminism, you discovered the "Goddess movement." How did that come about, and what the hell is it anyway?
I'm not going to get into the hostility to trans women that arose in the radical feminist world, but the Goddess movement was the rediscovery of the powerful female deities, temples, and stories before the rise of the so-called Great Religions.

Thank you for not telling us about your cats.
Anytime.

How would you describe your politics today?
Radical, sacred, hopefully magical.

Were you ever a Nice Jewish Boy?
I've always been Jewish, even when I thought I wasn't, and I'm pretty sure I've never been a boy, even when I thought I was. As for nice, I've always tried to be, but I've also always tried to be tough.

Bibliography

Novels

Golden Vanity (New York: Berkley Books, 1980)
Alqua Dreams (New York: Franklin Watts, 1987)
Unquenchable Fire (London: Century, 1988)
Temporary Agency (London: Orbit, 1994)
Godmother Night (New York: St. Martin's Press, 1996)
The Child Eater (New York: Quercus/Jo Fletcher Books, 2014)
The Fissure King: A Novel in Five Stories (Sumner, WA: Underland Press, 2017)

Collections

Burning Sky (Campbell, CA: Cambrian Publications, 1998)
The Tarot of Perfection: A Book of Tarot Tales (Prague: Magic Realist Press, 2008)

Poetry

Fortune's Lover (New York: A Midsummer Night's Press, 2009)

Translation

Tyrant Oidipous (Oedipus Rex), with David Vine (Roskilde: EyeCorner Press, 2012

Nonfiction

The Body of the Goddess (Shaftesbury: Element, 1997)

Tarot-related books

The Complete Illustrated Guide to Tarot (Shaftesbury: Element, 1999)

The Forest of Souls (St. Paul: Llewellyn, 2003)

Seventy-Eight Degrees of Wisdom, Part 1, The Major Arcana (Wellingborough: Aquarian Press, 1980); *Part 2, The Minor Arcana* (Wellingborough: Aquarian Press, 1983) Revised one-volume edition (London: HarperCollins, 1997)

Rachel Pollack's Tarot Wisdom (Woodbury, MN: Llewellyn, 2008)

The New Tarot Handbook (Woodbury, MN: Llewellyn, 2011)

Tarot and Oracle decks

Shining Woman Tarot, designed and drawn by Rachel Pollack (Wellingborough: Aquarian Press, 1992)

Shining Tribe Tarot, designed and drawn by Rachel Pollack (Woodbury, MN: Llewellyn, 2001)

The Burning Serpent Oracle, with artist Robert M. Place (Saugerties, NY: Hermes Publications, 2013)

The Raziel Tarot, with artist Robert M. Place (Saugerties, NY: Hermes Publications, 2016)

Comics

Doom Patrol (DC/Vertigo)

Tomahawk (DC/Vertigo)

The Geek (DC/Vertigo)

New Gods (DC)

Time Breakers (DC/Helix)

About the Author

RACHEL POLLACK IS THE author of forty-three books of fiction and nonfiction, including *Unquenchable Fire*, winner of the Arthur C. Clarke Award, and *Godmother Night*, winner of the World Fantasy Award. Her nonfiction includes a series of books on the spiritual and psychological symbolism in Tarot cards. Her Tarot book, *Seventy-Eight Degrees of Wisdom*, often described as "the bible of Tarot readers," has been in print continually since 1980 and has been sold around the world. Rachel is also a poet, author of the chapbook *Fortune's Lover*, and a visual artist, creator of the Shining Tribe Tarot deck. Working with the celebrated Tarot card artist Robert M. Place, she has created the Raziel Tarot, and the Burning Serpent Oracle. Rachel has taught and lectured in the U.S., Canada, Europe, Australia, New Zealand, and China. Her work has been translated into fifteen languages. For eleven years she was a senior faculty member of Goddard College's MFA writing program. Her most recent book is *The Fissure King: A Novel in Five Stories*.

FRIENDS OF PM

These are indisputably momentous times—the financial system is melting down globally and the Empire is stumbling. Now more than ever there is a vital need for radical ideas.

In the years since its founding—and on a mere shoestring—PM Press has risen to the formidable challenge of publishing and distributing knowledge and entertainment for the struggles ahead. With hundreds of releases to date, we have published an impressive and stimulating array of literature, art, music, politics, and culture. Using every available medium, we've succeeded in connecting those hungry for ideas and information to those putting them into practice.

Friends of PM allows you to directly help impact, amplify, and revitalize the discourse and actions of radical writers, filmmakers, and artists. It provides us with a stable foundation from which we can build upon our early successes and provides a much-needed subsidy for the materials that can't necessarily pay their own way. You can help make that happen—and receive every new title automatically delivered to your door once a month—by joining as a Friend of PM Press. And, we'll throw in a free T-shirt when you sign up.

Here are your options:
- $30 a month: Get all books and pamphlets plus 50% discount on all webstore purchases
- $40 a month: Get all PM Press releases (including CDs and DVDs) plus 50% discount on all webstore purchases
- $100 a month: Superstar—Everything plus PM merchandise, free downloads, and 50% discount on all webstore purchases

For those who can't afford $30 or more a month, we have Sustainer Rates at $15, $10, and $5. Sustainers get a free PM Press T-shirt and a 50% discount on all purchases from our website.

Your Visa or Mastercard will be billed once a month, until you tell us to stop. Or until our efforts succeed in bringing the revolution around. Or the financial meltdown of Capital makes plastic redundant. Whichever comes first.

PM Press was founded at the end of 2007 by a small collection of folks with decades of publishing, media, and organizing experience. PM Press co-conspirators have published and distributed hundreds of books, pamphlets, CDs, and DVDs. Members of PM have founded enduring book fairs, spearheaded victorious tenant organizing campaigns, and worked closely with bookstores, academic conferences, and even rock bands to deliver political and challenging ideas to all walks of life. We're old enough to know what we're doing and young enough to know what's at stake.

We seek to create radical and stimulating fiction and nonfiction books, pamphlets, T-shirts, visual and audio materials to entertain, educate, and inspire you. We aim to distribute these through every available channel with every available technology—whether that means you are seeing anarchist classics at our bookfair stalls; reading our latest vegan cookbook at the café; downloading geeky fiction e-books; or digging new music and timely videos from our website.

PM Press is always on the lookout for talented and skilled volunteers, artists, activists, and writers to work with. If you have a great idea for a project or can contribute in some way, please get in touch.

PM Press
PO Box 23912
Oakland, CA 94623
510-658-3906 • info@pmpress.org

PM Press in Europe
europe@pmpress.org
www.pmpress.org.uk

Report from Planet Midnight

Nalo Hopkinson
$12.00
ISBN: 978-1-60486-497-7
5 by 7.5 • 128 pages

Nalo Hopkinson has been busily (and wonderfully) "subverting the genre" since her first novel, *Brown Girl in the Ring*, won a Locus Award for SF and Fantasy in 1999. Since then she has acquired a prestigious World Fantasy Award, a legion of adventurous and aware fans, a reputation for intellect seasoned with humor, and a place of honor in the short list of SF writers who are tearing down the walls of category and transporting readers to previously unimagined planets and realms.

Never one to hold her tongue, Hopkinson takes on sexism and racism in publishing in "Report from Planet Midnight," a historic and controversial presentation to her colleagues and fans.

Plus... "Message in a Bottle," a radical new twist on the time travel tale that demolishes the sentimental myth of childhood innocence; and "Shift," a tempestuous erotic adventure in which Caliban gets the girl. Or does he?

And Featuring: our Outspoken Interview, an intimate one-on-one that delivers a wealth of insight, outrage, irreverence, and top-secret Caribbean spells.

Fire.

Elizabeth Hand
$13.00
ISBN: 978-1-62963-234-6
5 by 7.5 • 128 pages

The title story, "Fire." written especially for this volume, is a harrowing postapocalyptic adventure in a world threatened by global conflagration. Based on Hand's real-life experience as a participant in a governmental climate change think tank, it follows a ragtag cadre of scientists and artists racing to save both civilization and themselves from fast-moving global fires.

"The Woman Men Didn't See" is an expansion of Hand's acclaimed critical assessment of author Alice Sheldon, who wrote award-winning SF as "James Tiptree, Jr." in order to conceal identity from both the SF community and her CIA overlords. Another nonfiction piece, "Beyond Belief," recounts her difficult passage from alienated teen to serious artist.

Also included are "Kronia," a poignant time-travel romance, and "The Saffron Gatherers," two of Hand's favorite and less familiar stories. Plus: a bibliography and our candid and illuminating Outspoken Interview with one of today's most inventive authors.

PM PRESS PRESENTS

"A marvelous novel that moves beyond all preconceived categories."
—MARGARET RANDALL

CLANDESTINE
OCCUPATIONS

an imaginary history

DIANA BLOCK

Clandestine Occupations
An Imaginary History

Diana Block
$16.95
ISBN: 978-1-62963-121-9
5 by 8 • 256 pages

A radical activist, Luba Gold, makes the difficult decision to go underground to support the Puerto Rican independence movement. When Luba's collective is targeted by an FBI sting, she escapes with her baby but leaves behind a sensitive envelope that is being safeguarded by a friend. When the FBI come looking for Luba, the friend must decide whether to cooperate in the search for the woman she loves. Ten years later, when Luba emerges from clandestinity, she discovers that the FBI sting was orchestrated by another activist friend who had become an FBI informant. In the changed era of the 1990s, Luba must decide whether to forgive the woman who betrayed her.

Told from the points of view of five different women who cross paths with Luba over four decades, *Clandestine Occupations* explores the difficult decisions that activists confront about the boundaries of legality and speculates about the scope of clandestine action in the future. It is a thought-provoking reflection on the risks and sacrifices of political activism as well as the damaging reverberations of disaffection and cynicism.

Damnificados

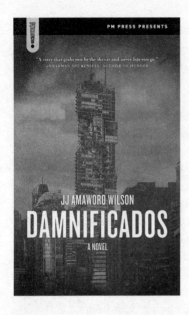

JJ Amaworo Wilson
$15.95
ISBN: 978-1-62963-117-2
5 by 8 • 288 pages

Damnificados is loosely based on the real-life occupation of a half-completed skyscraper in Caracas, Venezuela, the Tower of David. In this fictional version, six hundred "damnificados"—vagabonds and misfits—take over an abandoned urban tower and set up a community complete with schools, stores, beauty salons, bakeries, and a ragtag defensive militia. Their always heroic (and often hilarious) struggle for survival and dignity pits them against corrupt police, the brutal military, and the tyrannical "owners."

Taking place in an unnamed country at an unspecified time, the novel has elements of magical realism: avenging wolves, biblical floods, massacres involving multilingual ghosts, arrow showers falling to the tune of Beethoven's Ninth, and a trash truck acting as a Trojan horse. The ghosts and miracles woven into the narrative are part of a richly imagined world in which the laws of nature are constantly stretched and the past is always present.

> *"Should be read by every politician and rich bastard and then force-fed to them—literally, page by page."*
> —*Jimmy Santiago Baca, author of* A Place to Stand

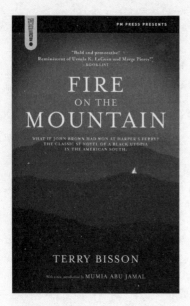

Fire on the Mountain

**Terry Bisson with an Introduction
by Mumia Abu-Jamal**
$15.95
ISBN: 978-1-60486-087-0
5 by 8 • 208 pages

It's 1959 in socialist Virginia. The Deep
South is an independent Black nation
called Nova Africa. The second Mars
expedition is about to touch down on
the red planet. And a pregnant scientist
is climbing the Blue Ridge in search of
her great-great grandfather, a teenage
slave who fought with John Brown
and Harriet Tubman's guerrilla army.

Long unavailable in the U.S., published in France as *Nova Africa*, *Fire on the
Mountain* is the story of what might have happened if John Brown's raid on
Harper's Ferry had succeeded—and the Civil War had been started not by
the slave owners but the abolitionists.

> *"History revisioned, turned inside out ... Bisson's
> wild and wonderful imagination has taken some
> strange turns to arrive at such a destination."*
> —*Madison Smartt Bell, Anisfield-Wolf Award
> winner and author of* Devil's Dream